A Ghost of a Chance

THE GHOST DETECTIVE MYSTERIES - BOOK 4

JANE HINCHEY

BAYWOLF PRESS
BP
BAYWOLF PRESS

ACKNOWLEDGEMENTS

A wholehearted thank-you to my insider team, Misty, Fleur, Dana, Lilly, and Marcia. You have been my biggest fans and greatest supporters. I couldn't have done 2020 without you.

To my ARC Team for devouring my words with such relish and always being eager for more, despite the incredibly short notice I give you *most* of the time. Thank you.

To my fabulous readers group, Jane's Little Devils, you guys are the best. Thanks for hanging out with me, sharing pics of your pets and generally enjoying my crazy.

To my family. Thank you. I love you.

And finally, my readers. Thank you for picking up this book and for taking a chance on me :)

xoxo
Jane

AUTHOR'S NOTE

Hey! Welcome to the weird and wacky world of my imagination. I hope you enjoy your time here.

If you love anything supernatural as much as I do, then you're going to enjoy the journey ahead - at least I think you will.

Give up the Ghost is the second book in my Ghost Detective series, with more to come, so make sure you sign up for my newsletter to get notifications on when the next book is ready.

You can sign up for my newsletter here: **Janehinchey.com/subscribe**

Okay, ready to weave some magic and solve some mysteries?

I'll see you on the other side!

xoxo

Jane

FREE BOOK OFFER

Want to get an email alert when the next Ghost Detective Mystery is available? Sign up for my newsletter today, https://janehinchey.com/subscribe and as a bonus, receive a FREE e-book of **Cupcakes & Curses!**

ABOUT THIS BOOK

Running a private investigation business in the seaside town of Firefly Bay should be a pretty easy job. One where I call the shots—figuratively speaking because to put clumsy little ole me in charge of a firearm is just asking for trouble. After a hectic few months, all I'm after is an easy day, where my cases add up to nothing more strenuous than deciding if tonight's takeout is pizza or tacos (or both).

Should have known my day was going to go to hell in a handbasket when someone switched out my coffee for decaf (seriously, who does that?) and my main squeeze, Captain Cowboy Hot Pants, aka Detective Kade Galloway's ex-girlfriend and internal affairs investigator, Savannah Mcintosh, turns up to work a case.

Before I can say café latte, Galloway's dodging my calls, I've got a raccoon on my hands who's decided mi casa es su casa, my ghostly best friend has a crush to die for, and local teenager Kira Meléndez has turned up missing.

So much for an easy day. I have a sneaking suspicion my life is about to become a whole new level of crazy.

Chapter One

Pushing down the knot of dread in my chest, I wondered, yet again, if I were ready to face what this day had to throw at me. I had been summoned to Firefly Bay Police Department to give a formal statement regarding my encounters with Officer Ian Mills. Mills, in my opinion, was a dirty cop, and I didn't make that allegation lightly. Not after what happened to my best friend and former detective, Ben Delaney.

Ben was framed by a dodgy co-worker and ultimately forced out of the career he'd loved. And that had started my love-hate relationship with the police. Hate for what they'd done to Ben, love because now I was dating a super-hot cop, Detective Kade Galloway, aka *Captain Cowboy Hot Pants*.

I know. I'm as surprised as you are, to be honest. I mean me? Date a cop? Ludicrous. But I guess stranger things have happened —believe me, they really have! It helped that Galloway was involved in a secret investigation into corrupt law enforcement officials. Now, after months of what looked like little to no progress, an internal affairs investigator had turned up. The entire station was in an uproar, except for Galloway, who was in on the whole thing. And the IA investigator, obviously.

Blowing on my cup of joe, I looked out the back window toward the woods that bordered one side of my property. It still felt odd to think of this house and land as mine. It was Ben's. Only he'd died months ago, leaving me... everything. His house. His car— let's not get into me totaling it one night while being chased by gun-wielding bad guys. The good news is I got a new car. It's a metallic, sporty blue Honda CR-V, and it is *divine*. I also inherited Ben's private investigation business, and that's how I ended up here. It felt like a dream, but I really was a brand-new PI, with a beautiful house and a healthy bank balance.

"Second thoughts?" Ben's ghost appeared by my side, startling me. I jerked, and coffee sloshed over the rim of my cup.

"Dude!" I snapped, giving him the side-eye. "How many times?"

"I can't help it! I'm a ghost. I make zero noise."

I took a sip of the scalding liquid, ignoring the spill but promising myself I'd wipe it up later, and eyeballed the thick clouds rolling in. A storm was coming. Not only could I see it in the gray skies outside the window, but I also felt it in my bones. Dark and ominous. Either that or I had arthritis, and I'd like to think that I was too young for such an affliction at twenty-nine. I stared at the hand not holding the coffee cup then opened and closed my fist a couple of times. I stretched my fingers out until I felt the pull and strain on muscles and tendons before curling them back in tight. Nope. No pain. Not arthritis, then.

"What *are* you doing?" Ben asked.

"Checking for arthritis," I replied absently, my eyes drifting back to the woods. That's where he'd died. Where I'd found his body.

Ben followed my gaze and sighed. We'd been over this countless times. Ben had had the opportunity to cross over but had opted to stay, and I worried. I worried that he'd committed to living his life as a ghost. The only person who could see him and communicate with him was me. Was that enough? And then I worried that he'd eventually leave. I'd long since decided that ghost Ben was better than no Ben at all, and despite not being happy about his death, I'd accepted that this was our new normal.

And as my best friend, Ben sometimes knew me better than I knew myself. "Worried about Galloway's new partner?"

I lifted one shoulder in a half-hearted shrug. *Good question.* But not the right question. Somewhere between last night's karaoke rendition of *Man, I Feel Like A Woman* and my sixth shot of tequila, I'd hit upon what was really bugging me, and despite appearances, it was not Savannah Mcintosh.

Savannah was the IA investigator sent to unravel the secrets and lies permeating Firefly Bay's law enforcement department. She was tall, blonde, blue-eyed, and supermodel drop-dead gorgeous. She was also Galloway's ex. Everyone thought I should be threatened by her presence. The expectation was that I'd be filled with a mad woman's level of jealousy and dutifully act all crazy about it. I never was any good at living up to expectations.

Okay, fine. Last night's hoorah at the pub had been the culmination of too many long days and sleepless nights and had nothing to do with Savannah's arrival. I'd been on a case. A stakeout, to be precise. My client, Mrs. Morgan, had hired me to get to the bottom of her disappearing newspaper. I know it doesn't sound exciting, and to be truthful, it wasn't. But it was a case, and it gave me something to do. Business had been quiet of late, so beggars couldn't be choosers, and finding missing pets and stolen newspapers stopped me from overthinking... stuff.

It hadn't been a difficult case to crack. Kind of predictable, really. Still, it had meant staking out Mrs. Morgan's house for several early mornings in a row before I caught the culprit—her neighbor being liberal with that term, of course—red-handed. In fact, I'd gotten it all on camera. Video evidence of the thief creeping across Mrs. Morgan's front lawn in the early hours to relieve her of the newspaper the delivery boy had expertly tossed onto her front doormat. I'd delivered my final report to Mrs. Morgan, and the case was closed. What she chose to do about her thieving neighbor was on her. My involvement ended the minute I solved the mystery.

So, yes, tying one on had been partly celebratory but mostly to dull the twinge of annoyance that everyone—my family included—expected me to throw a hissy fit over Savannah's arrival and apparent history with Galloway. But I'd never been the jealous type, and now was no exception. No, the truth was, my concerns weren't about Savannah and Galloway at all. They revolved around the deposition itself.

This was the opportunity I'd been both anticipating and dreading. So much rode on my testimony. There was nothing I wanted more than to see Mills prosecuted to the full extent of the law. I knew there was more to the investigation than Mills and me, though. Galloway had said the corruption went high up the food chain. Mills was a small cog in a much bigger machine. My worry was that if I somehow botched this, Mills would get off scot-free, and that would have a snowball effect. Like a house of cards, the entire investigation would come crashing down.

The rational part of my brain told me that was unlikely, but still, the worry niggled at me. That anxiety, plus the fact that the worry itself irked me, was enough to cause a tiny bout of hyperventilation every time I thought about it.

"I'm not worried about Savannah Mcintosh."

"Gotta say, she's hot." Ben squared his shoulders and puffed out his chest. "If I were corporeal..."

I snorted. "Right. Have at her, hot stuff. I'm sure she'd love you ghosting her every move." I giggled at my own pun, then sobered. "Actually, that's not such a bad idea."

"You want me to spy on her? Fitz, that's not like you."

"What do you mean that's not like me? That's exactly like me."

He smirked. "Yeah, you're right. So… you want me to see what she and Kade are up to?"

I frowned. "What are you talking about? No. I do not want you to spy on my boyfriend. *Geez, Ben.* I want you to find out how the investigation is going. Honestly, everyone seems to be fixated on me, Galloway, and *her,* when y'all should be focusing on what she's here for."

Ben had the grace to look contrite. "You're right. Sorry. Focus on the case."

"Right," I grumbled, eyeing my cup suspiciously. Usually, I'd have felt the effects of caffeination by now. My early morning irritability would be easing, not rising. I took another sip, the hot brew bitter on my tongue.

"What time is your deposition?" Ben asked.

"Nine."

"You know it's eight-thirty, right?"

I almost dropped my cup. "No way." I turned to look at the massive clock on the living room wall. "See? Seven-thirty."

"Fitz. That clock stopped working last week. I told you about it. Haven't you noticed every time you look at it, it says seven-thirty?"

No, no, no. Hurrying to the kitchen, I slammed my coffee onto the counter and picked up my phone to double-check. *Eight-thirty.* With a shriek, I let the phone clatter back to the counter and sprinted for the stairs, Ben hot on my heels.

"Don't panic. You already picked out what you're going to wear, right?"

"Yes!" I'd chosen black. Sharp. Mysterious. Slightly menacing. And it hid any stains. When I waved my finger and twirled it in the air, Ben dutifully stopped following and turned his back. We'd worked out a system, of sorts, so he wouldn't surprise me naked. Nothing worse than a pervy ghost.

Stripping out of my PJs, I shimmied into clean underwear, spritzed deodorant under my arms, then pulled on black pants, a white T-shirt (turned around, so the stain was at the back), and a black blazer. After sliding my feet into black patent heels, I hurried into the bathroom. No time to give my makeup the attention my face deserved. Rather than the immaculate winged eyeliner I'd been planning on, with the classic red lip, I wiped a handful of BB cream across my face and a smear of lip gloss.

My hair was its usual disaster, a collar length blonde wavy bob, but my hairstylist was a genius who cut it in such a way the messy style looked like I'd spent hours in the bathroom achieving it. And that only came about because I'd burned a good chunk of hair off with a curling iron, so the shorter style was the only recourse.

I patted my hair and tugged on my lapels. "I do look rather badass, don't I?"

"All that matters is that *you* think you look badass," Ben said, leaning against the doorjamb. I flipped him the bird and hurried back downstairs, twisting my ankle on the last step and only just stopping myself from sprawling in an undignified heap on the floor.

"Careful," Ben cautioned. "Are you sure the heels are a good idea?"

My ankle throbbed, but I refused to admit Ben was right. The heels were a ridiculous idea. I was the clumsiest person I knew. If it were possible to trip over air, I'd do it. As it was, heels were usually a big no-no, but today I felt in need of courage in the form of a badass outfit. And that included heels.

"Are you nervous?" he asked.

I lifted a shoulder. "No. I don't know. Maybe."

"Decisive as ever, Fitz. You'll be fine. Now, do you have everything?"

I frowned. "I think so."

"Keys?"

I patted my pocket. Empty. Hobbling into the open plan living area, I snatched up the keys from the coffee table, my phone from the kitchen counter, then swung around, searching for my purse.

"By the front door. Where you dropped it when you came in last night." Ben always did have a knack for knowing what I was thinking. Well, most times. Sometimes he got it spectacularly wrong.

"Right." Walking as fast as my twisted ankle allowed, I made my way to the front of the house. Sure enough, there was my purse on the floor by the front door.

Snatching it up, I tossed my phone inside, slung the bag over my shoulder, and made my way to the garage and my Honda CR-V. It was a little worrisome how much I loved this car. Maybe because it was the first brand new car I'd ever bought? My last car had been a rusted-out Chrysler, circa 1970. Then I'd briefly had possession of Ben's Nissan Rogue, but that had been *Ben's* car—it wasn't the same. But the Honda was all mine. I lovingly stroked my hand along the paintwork before opening the door and sliding behind the wheel.

"Just take it easy on the road, okay, Fitz?" Ben said from the passenger seat.

"You're already dead; you can't die again," I pointed out, hitting the button for the automatic garage door opener and starting the engine.

"True. But you can."

"My driving is *not* that bad!" I shot him a look, then backed out of the drive. Spring was in the air, despite the storm that was rolling in. Little green buds of leaves dotted the trees, and plants I didn't know were in my garden were starting to poke their heads through the soil, preparing for sunshine and glorious days.

I drove down the street, sunny skies ahead. Dark, voluminous clouds in my rearview warned of a storm approaching. A crack of thunder boomed, and a shiver danced over my skin.

"I hope this isn't a sign," I whispered, my eyes darting from the rearview to the windshield and back again.

"Of what? Impending doom?" Ben grinned. "Relax, Fitz. It's just a storm. They happen, on account of the weather. It has absolutely nothing to do with your deposition today."

Pulling my mouth into a straight line, I could only hope he was right.

Chapter Two

Thanks to the joys of small-town living, I pulled up in front of FBPD five minutes later. Putting the Honda into park, I turned off the ignition and turned to my incorporeal friend in the passenger seat. "I have a favor to ask."

"Oh?"

"Do not come into the interview room with me. Ben, I love you to bits, but you are a distraction, and I know you'll mean to help..." I blew out a breath. "I do not need

Savannah thinking I'm some sort of looney tune who talks to thin air. If I get caught talking to you, that's what she's going to think. And then my testimony will be worth nothing because she won't believe me. She'll probably suggest a psych evaluation."

Ben propped an elbow on the armrest and looked at me. "Fine. I won't come in."

"But poke around the rest of the station," I offered.

"And check in on Galloway."

I groaned. "I did not say that."

"You didn't have to."

A sharp rap at my window startled me. Peering through the window, I saw a brown-haired, gray-eyed, tall Caucasian in black jeans, a gray T-shirt, and a black suit jacket wearing a grin that weakened my knees.

Opening the door, I fell out of the car and into his arms. He squeezed me tight and twirled me in a circle, and I squealed like a schoolgirl, all badassery out the window.

"I've missed you," Galloway said, setting me back on my feet.

"I've missed you too." We'd both been busy. Him with the investigation, me with missing newspapers.

He gestured toward the building. "You ready for this?"

My stomach did somersaults. *Was* I ready for this? Galloway had warned me there could be ramifications. When heads started to roll—and he was sure they would—officers would lose their jobs. Their pensions. Lives would be affected. Small-town rumors would be running hot. And Mills would blame me, but nothing new there. He blamed me for his suspension while the investigation was underway anyway.

My mind flashed back to the day Anita Finley had died out at the Kelsh Estate. I'd discovered her body, and Officer Ian Mills and Sergeant Dwight Clements had attended. There had always been tension between Mills and me. I was sure he'd busted out my taillight on purpose, just so he could book me. I was sure it was him who'd broken into my apartment and trashed it, then knocked me over the upstairs landing when I'd interrupted him. Only I couldn't prove any of that. What I could prove was the physical assault on the day of Anita's death.

He'd lost his mind that day. Apparently, I'd pushed him over the edge, his temper had snapped, and he'd attacked. I had the bruises around my neck and his skin under my nails as proof. But I knew all too well that evidence could disappear, and statements could be tampered with.

"I'm ready." I wasn't. I felt sure I was going to puke. Sweat beaded on my brow, my mouth went dry, and my stomach flip-flopped some more.

"Audrey?" Galloway rested a hand on my shoulder and peered into my face. "You've got this. I don't know why you're so nervous. Just tell Savannah everything you know about Mills. That's it. Look, I've told you before. He's small fry in all of this, but he could be our ticket to busting up the corruption plaguing the FBPD by giving us names of others involved. He's not the only one under suspicion."

"Yes, but he's the only one who's been publicly named. Everyone knows he attacked me, that he would have happily killed me if I hadn't beamed him with that rock. Even

Clements was surprised at the level of violence."

"Take a breath." He pulled me against his chest, smothering my face. I was grateful I hadn't gone with the winged eyeliner now, for it would surely have been smeared across his shirt. "Everything will be fine."

Sliding my arms underneath his jacket and around his waist, I basked in his warmth, my nerves settling somewhat. "Can we go in together? Or is that fraternization?"

Chuckling, he released me and grabbed hold of my hand, leading me toward the station's front door. "Of course we can go in together. Everyone knows you're my girlfriend."

I still got a kick out of hearing it, and I still had no idea how it had happened, but I was glad it had. Galloway had been a breath of fresh air and sunshine on an otherwise rainy day.

Inside, it was business as usual. Desks took up most of the main room. A glass wall separated the public entrance and the administration area upfront. As soon as we'd stepped over the threshold, the sound of typing and papers shuffling amplified, and I figured they'd all been spying on us out front.

Sergeant Addison Young leaned back in her chair and threw me a smile. "Hey, Audrey. Good to see you again."

My mouth was dry again, and my lips stuck to my teeth when I returned her smile, which I'm sure came off more like baring my teeth at her. Addison winked, then turned back to her desk, resuming typing.

"Audrey." Officer Noah Walsh approached, holding two cups of coffee. He placed one on the corner of Addison's desk and took a sip of the other. My eyes narrowed in on the cup. *I'd kill for a coffee.*

I was still daydreaming about coffee when I realized work had come to a complete standstill, and the FBPD staff were all looking over my right shoulder. I didn't have to turn around to know that Internal Affairs Investigator Savannah Mcintosh had entered the room.

"Audrey Fitzgerald?" The dulcet tones that reached my ears could have been from a phone sex operator if I knew what one even sounded like. But I'd imagined it would be like the warm, honeyed tones coming from behind me.

I turned. I'd seen Savannah from a distance before, so her beauty shouldn't have come as such a shock. But up close? Up close, she was amazingly magnificent. As expected, she wore a suit—a navy blue stripe, the jacket done up at the waist with two buttons, the cut accentuating the slimness of her waist and curve of her hips. Beneath the jacket was a crisp white blouse. On her feet, peek-toe black heels.

Her long blonde hair cascaded over her shoulders in a dead straight waterfall of gorgeousness. Seriously, her hair should be in shampoo commercials. Her blue eyes were accentuated with a coat of mascara and subtle blending of eyeliner, her lips sported a nude shade of lipstick. Her skin was so clear she could have been airbrushed. Understated, elegant, stylish.

Straightening my shoulders, I took a step forward and held out my hand. "Savannah. Pleased to meet you."

Her handshake was firm, her smile warm. "Come on through. Kade, could you get us a couple of coffees?"

"Sure."

I threw him a glance over my shoulder as I followed Savannah to an interview room. Seemed like he didn't mind being an errand boy for his ex. But then, why would he? There was no way Galloway would be pining after little Miss Universe here... because he had me, and I was plenty woman enough for any man. It wouldn't hurt him to bring us coffee though, keep him humble.

"Good luck," he said to me before joining the others, who were currently hovering around the coffeepot like they weren't remotely interested in the meeting of the girlfriends, current and ex.

Then I saw Ben, mouth hanging open, eyeballs out on stalks as he ogled Savannah. I dropped my head, dread flooding me. He was going to mess this up for me, I just knew it. I tried to get his attention, but he only had eyes for the tall blonde. My stomach returned to flip-flopping, and an uncomfortable wave of perspiration broke out, making me thankful for the dark jacket that would hide any pit stains.

"Fitz, I'm sorry!" Ben apologized for the millionth time, and I continued to ignore him. "Look… she just… she's…" he blathered, as he had been since laying eyes on Savannah Mcintosh. Once an articulate and, dare I say, intelligent ghost, he'd now become a mumbling, bumbling idiot.

He'd followed us into the interview room—despite promising that he would do no such thing—and had simply *stared* at Savannah the entire time, with a dreamy expression on his face, hanging on her every word.

"I guess I should be grateful you kept your mouth shut," I conceded, tossing my purse onto the kitchen counter and kicking off my shoes. My ankle was turning lovely shades of blue and purple, and I rotated it to see if it still hurt. It did. The movement sent a sharp bolt of pain up my leg.

"Wow." Ben crouched to get a closer look. "I didn't realize it was that bad. You should ice it."

"Thanks, genius," I grumbled, reaching for the coffee cup I'd abandoned that morning, the contents long since cold. I considered my options. Zap it in the microwave or make a fresh cup. Then I looked a little closer at the brown liquid. Was that a... *cat hair?*

"Thor!" I bellowed. The big, gray teddy bear of a cat that I'd inherited from Ben squeezed through the cat door, his orange eyes landing on me.

"Oh good, you're back," he said in his adorable British accent.

"Don't tell me. You're starving," I said sarcastically. It was Thor's catch cry, and I was starting to think I needed to pull back on responding quite so readily. Soon he wouldn't even fit through the cat door at all. I pointed to my coffee cup. "Have you been drinking my coffee?"

"Why would I do that?" He sat, licked a paw, then rubbed it over his face.

"Don't think you can fool me," I warned. "Answering a question with a question is a dead giveaway." Thor paused in his grooming and eyeballed me.

Then, with a slow blink, he resumed washing himself. Around a mouthful of fur, he said, "Fine. It smelled different. I wanted to check."

"Check? Check what? Wait! You don't think it was poisoned, do you?" I hadn't drunk much of it that morning, but maybe it was enough to make me break out in a sweat and feel nauseous. Maybe my earlier reaction hadn't been nerves at all.

"Relax, Sherlock. Who'd want to poison you?"

"Well, I don't know! Anyone!" I snapped my fingers and pointed at Thor. "Mills! Ian Mills would like to see me dead, I'm sure."

"That may well be, but your coffee wasn't poisoned."

"What, then?"

"It's decaf."

It started with a ringing in my ears that slowly got louder and louder. My eyes locked on Thor as he sat washing his cute face as if he hadn't just dropped the biggest bombshell in the world. "It's what?" I choked out, hand going to my throat.

"Whoa." Ben sounded equally horrified. "You sure?"

Thor's tail slapped the floor. "Of course, I'm sure."

I fanned my face. "Wait. Let me get this clear. You're telling me someone has switched my coffee out for decaf?"

Thor tilted his head and considered. "I can't say someone switched it out. Maybe you bought the wrong coffee. But I can say with one hundred percent conviction that that coffee is decaf."

Flinging open the overhead cupboard, I pulled down the box of Folgers Classic Roast. Despite having Ben's fancy pants coffee machine, I still loved my Keurig and used the K-cup pods religiously. I was a press-one-button- and-the-magic-brew appeared kinda girl.

I opened the lid and bit back a gasp. My Folgers Classic Roast K-cups had been replaced with Folgers 100% Colombian *decaffeinated* coffee.

"Argh!" I yelled, snatching up a pod and throwing it across the room. "Who did this?"

Ben held up his hands and backed away. "Hey! It wasn't me."

I snorted. "I didn't think it was you, genius. You can't pick anything up. Who had the nerve to come into my house and switch my coffee behind my back? And how did I not know about it?"

"You're missing the obvious question," Thor said.

"What's that?" I tossed the box of pods in the trash.

"*Why* would someone do that?"

Good question. The why would lead to the who. Crossing my arms, I stared at the floor, deep in thought. I could only assume whoever had done this was concerned for my health. They thought I drank too much coffee. And knowing I would not respond well to anyone suggesting I cut back my caffeine intake...

I pulled the phone out of my purse and dialed. "Mom, how could you!"

"Audrey? What do you mean? What's happened?"

"You know what's happened," I accused. "Decaf! How could you?" There was a moment's silence.

"Audrey, love, I really don't know what you're talking about. Decaf? What? You're telling me you've switched to decaf? I mean, that's great, I guess?"

"You mean it wasn't you?"

"You're not making any sense."

"Did you or did you not switch out my coffee pods for decaf?"

I could have sworn I heard her giggle.

"I did not."

Darn. Not Mom. She'd have fessed up by now. But it had to be another family member. "I bet it was Dustin," I snapped. "Playing another of his practical jokes." Oh, that brother of mine would pay big time for this one. "Sorry, Mom, gotta go. I'm out of coffee."

"I thought you just said someone switched out your coffee for decaf? How can you be out?"

"Duh, I can't drink decaf. What's the point? I need to go to the store and re-stock. Clearly, I'm going to have to start storing my beverage of choice under lock and key."

After finishing up the call with Mom and promising her I'd be at the family dinner (all the while plotting revenge on my brother), I hobbled toward the front door, pointing an accusing finger at Ben as I passed. "Don't think you're off the hook."

"No, ma'am." He had the grace to look suitably chastised. I knew he wasn't, of course. And considering he made no move to join me, I figured as soon as I'd driven away, he'd be heading back to the station to follow Savannah around. And honestly, I probably wouldn't mind—much—if it meant he'd find out anything useful. Instead, I knew he'd be following her like a lovesick ghost, which was kinda pervy and gross.

Chapter Three

Garrido Bodega was a transplant from New York City, as was its owner, Nick Garrido. The little Hispanic grocery store held a ton of products in a tiny space and was my go-to when I only needed a couple of items and was in a hurry. I pulled up as close as possible to the door and then hobbled inside, my ankle twinging in protest with each step. The rapid swelling had meant I couldn't squeeze my foot back into my heels, so here I was in my badass suit with flip flops. *Killing it in the fashion department, Fitz.*

"Hey, Nick." I waved to the fifty-year-old Latino behind the counter. "How goes it?"

"Audrey, you're looking sharp today."

"Right?" I grinned. "You got any of those ankle strap things?"

He bustled around from behind the counter. "What have you done, *amigas*?"

We both looked at my discolored foot. "You know me. Always tripping over or banging into something."

He shook his head, probably wondering how one person could constantly have such bad luck then led me down an aisle stocked high with dog food. "Ah, *gringa*, your mother must despair."

"I'm sure she does."

Halfway down the aisle between the dog food and feminine hygiene products was a small supply of first aid items. Nick grabbed an ACE wrap and tossed it at me. It bounced off my chest and fell to the floor, where we both looked at it for a second before bursting out laughing.

Composing myself, I bent and picked it up. "Thanks."

"No problemo. Anything else for you today?"

"Just coffee, but I know where that is."

Nick took the ACE wrap from me, shuffling back toward the counter. "I'll ring this up before you drop it again."

Hurrying as fast as my dodgy ankle would allow, I found my coffee, grabbed two boxes in case the coffee-switcher-outerer struck again, and made my way to the register to pay.

Nick eyed the two boxes of coffee. "Big case?"

"You wouldn't believe it, but someone switched out my coffee for decaf!"

He froze, fingers hovering over the till, eyes round. "No!" he gasped.

I nodded sadly. "Yup. I don't know what the world is coming to."

He finished ringing me up, took my cash, and bagged the coffee and bandage. "I hear you, *chero*, I hear you."

"I'm going to hide one of these, just in case the nefarious switcher-outerer strikes again."

Nick grinned then winked. "Smart."

"Thanks." Taking the bag, I waved and hobbled to the door, only as I was about to step out, someone else was stepping in, and we collided with an oomph.

"Good grief, Audrey! What are you wearing?"

"Amanda, hi," I greeted my sister-in-law. Amanda was the stunningly beautiful, incredibly smart, accomplished wife of my brother, Dustin. Not only was she the perfect mom to my niece and nephew, Madeline and Nathaniel, but she also worked full time as a paralegal at Beasley, Tate & Associates.

Amanda was on a quest to fix me. She considered my clumsiness a major flaw and basically thought I had a screw loose in my gray matter, and if I only got professional help (aka see a shrink), my clumsiness would magically disappear. It was a sore point between us. And it wasn't that I didn't love Amanda. I did, but...

"Never mind, I probably don't want to know." She dragged her eyes up from my flip flops to focus on my face. "Actually, I'm glad I caught you."

"Oh?" I clutched the grocery bag to my chest and eyed the Honda CR-V. I wasn't in the mood to stand around and chat, not with a painful ankle and a severe caffeine deficiency.

"I may have a case for you." She dug in her purse, pulled out a card, and handed it to me.

"Ivelisse Day Spa," I read aloud. "Isn't that the new place that recently opened? In a renovated house or something?"

"Yes. Stephanie Melendez purchased the old Bailey house and refurbished it. Beasley, Tate & Associates handled the sale and rezoning."

"Right. What's the case?" *Please don't say missing newspapers.*

"It might not be anything, but I happened to be at the spa this morning when there was a bit of a fuss."

"A bit of a fuss? What does that mean?"

"Well, apparently, Stephanie's daughter, Kira, didn't turn up for track practice."

I blinked. "Ummm. Okay. How old is Kira?"

"Fifteen."

"Right. A fifteen-year-old didn't show up for practice? I'd say she's either hanging with friends or at the mall."

"That's what I said to her mom," Amanda agreed. "But Stephanie wasn't convinced. She says Kira is an outstanding athlete with a real passion for track and field. She has her eye set on the Olympics. She says Kira would never miss training. Never."

"And I assume she's done the usual? Called all Kira's friends?"

Amanda nodded. "Yes. No one has seen her. Stephanie thinks she's missing."

"Has she called the police?"

"Yes, but they didn't seem concerned. They said it's only been a couple of hours and given her age…"

"They think she's just messing around." She probably was. I looked at the card in my hand. I had no active cases. With Galloway tied up at work, it couldn't hurt to look into Kira's apparent disappearance.

"Okay, I'll give Stephanie a call."

Amanda beamed at me. "Excellent. I told her you would."

Wait. Amanda had told them I'd take the case before speaking with me, which would have been easy enough to do by simply picking up the phone. Instead, I'd bumped into her here, at the Bodega. A place where I imagined Amanda would never shop.

"I'll let you get back to your shopping." I stood aside and motioned for her to go past. Her eyes darted from me to the eclectically stocked grocery store behind me. "Nick's is great, isn't it?" I continued. "You can get almost anything here. What is it that you're after?"

A flush of color bloomed on her cheekbones. "Oh. Um. Ah." I could see she was casting around for a suitable lie. I waited patiently, not letting her off the hook. "Spices!" she finally blurted.

"Nice." I grinned. "Nick has a great range, don't you, Nick?" I called over my shoulder.

"What's that, *gringa*?" Nick lifted his head from reading the newspaper laid out on the counter.

"Nick, this is my sister-in-law, Amanda. She's after some spices."

"Oh, pretty lady, Nick has all the spices you need," Nick declared. "Come, come, I show you." With arms waving, he ushered Amanda inside, and I slipped out, moving as fast as my sprained ankle would allow. Inside my car, I tossed the grocery bag on the passenger seat, started the engine, then dialed Stephanie's number, connecting the call via Bluetooth.

One more glance through the window at Nick gesturing wildly as he regaled Amanda with the delights of his Bodega, and I pulled away. *Serves her right for lying to me.* What had me puzzled was *why*? Why track me down, at the Garrido Bodega of all places, just to tell me about a potential case? Especially when a phone call would have done the trick?

"Ivelisse Day Spa, Stephanie speaking, how can I help you today?"

"Oh, hi. This is Audrey Fitzgerald from Delaney Investigations," I began, turning my attention to the road and the call.

"Thank you so much for calling. Amanda said you might."

I frowned. What was Amanda up to? Was she in cahoots with my brother over this whole decaffeinated coffee business? Was she trying to lure me out of the house, keep me distracted so he could slip in and switch out something else? Mental note—check he hadn't switched my milk to low fat. "I understand your daughter is missing?"

"I know it sounds crazy. Kira was supposed to be at training at eleven. When she didn't show, Coach called me."

I glanced at the clock on my dash. Quarter past twelve. Hardly any reason to panic.

"Eleven is a bit of an odd hour for training, isn't it? I thought track was after school."

"This is a special program, only for the most talented and gifted students. And Kira is not only that, but she's also dedicated. There is no way she'd miss class."

"Did she turn up to school at all today?"

There was a pause. "You know, I didn't even think to check," Stephanie admitted.

"That's okay. Why don't you give the school a call? And if it's okay with you, I'll drop in to meet with you in person. You can give me a picture of Kira, and we can find out what your daughter is up to. By the time I arrive, we should know if she went to school at all."

"Yes. Yes, thank you." The note of relief in her voice was unmistakable. Disconnecting the call, I thrummed my thumb on the steering wheel. Assuming Kira *was* missing and not ditching school, it made all the difference just how long she'd been gone. How far could one teenager get with a three-and-a-half-hour lead?

The Ivelisse Day Spa was gorgeous, a charming historic mansion that was once a bed and breakfast but had been renovated into a day spa thanks to Beasley, Tate & Associates' client, Stephanie Melendez. Leaving my shopping in the car, I limped up the red brick path toward the two-story building. It was white on white, with large arched windows.

"Only just opened for business, still fixing the finer details," I said to myself, eyeing the gardeners who were busy raking the lawn and hastily seeing to last-minute plantings along the garden bed bordering the front veranda. A quaint sign was currently being erected on the front lawn. Two men in overalls were washing the enormous front windows.

Pushing open the glossy wooden door, I stepped into the foyer. There was a reception area directly ahead, a refreshments area to the right, and a cozy seating nook to the left. Everything was new and fresh and oh so beautiful. A woman looked up from behind the reception desk. "Audrey?" she asked.

"At your service."

"Welcome to Ivelisse Day Spa." The smile was forced. "I'm Stephanie Melendez."

"I have to ask, what does Ivelisse mean?"

Stephanie's mouth twisted into a grimace of a smile. "It means life."

I nodded. "Nice place. You haven't been open long, right?"

"We opened on Monday, and the grand opening party is next week. Assuming…"

Assuming her daughter turned up.

"Is there somewhere we can talk?"

"Come through to my office."

I followed her through a set of French doors. The styling in the office was simple but elegant, much like Stephanie herself. She wore pale pink scrubs. Her blonde hair was pulled up into a high ponytail, and her blue eyes were adorned with a brush of mascara and just a hint of bronze eyeshadow.

I took the seat opposite the desk and waited while she fiddled with her phone. "Here," she said, holding it toward me, "this is Kira."

I leaned forward and looked at the picture of the smiling teenager. She was definitely of mixed heritage. She had her mother's stunning blue eyes. I assumed her father was Hispanic, given the olive skin, dark brown hair, and Melendez's surname.

"She's beautiful."

Stephanie turned the phone back and looked at the photo of her daughter. "She is." A moment's silence followed as Stephanie plunged into memories of her daughter and dread at her apparent disappearance.

I cleared my throat. "Could you send me that? My number should be in your call log."

Shaking herself out of her thoughts, she swiped the screen. "Sure." Seconds later, my phone dinged, announcing the arrival of a message. I didn't bother looking at it.

"How did it go with the school?" I asked.

Stephanie's face fell, and she shook her head. "Kira didn't go to any of her classes."

"And you didn't receive a truancy notification?"

She shook her head again. "No. Which is odd."

"When was the last time you saw her?"

"This morning at breakfast. She walks to school, so she leaves around eight-fifteen."

"And nothing unusual happened this morning? She took her school bag as usual? Wasn't wearing anything out of character?"

"Everything was... normal. She wore jeans and a T-shirt and a school sweater. She had her backpack."

It looked like Kira Melendez had left for school that morning, as usual, only she hadn't arrived.

"Could you write me down a list of Kira's friends and places she likes to hang out? Oh, and the coach's info if you have it. I know you've already spoken to everyone you can think of. Still, I'll circle back around and see if anyone remembers anything."

"The police didn't seem that worried. They said she'd only been missing such a short amount of time that it was most likely nothing. That she'd turn up."

I reached across the desk and patted her hand in a soothing gesture. "I know. But we have to remember that the police are contacted for missing teenagers more frequently than they'd probably like. And nine times out of ten, those missing teenagers aren't exactly missing. They're either ditching school or ditching their parents and, well, just being teenagers, really. But if Kira was a toddler? You can bet they'd be all over this."

"I guess."

I rose from my seat. "Try not to worry. We'll get your daughter back."

"What happens now?"

"I'll make some calls, go visit Coach, drop in at the school, that type of thing. If she hasn't turned up by close of business then I'll come to your house and speak with you and your husband." I paused. "Nothing's happened at home?"

"Between Bill and I? No, we're good. The only thing that has changed is me getting this place up and running. It's taken a lot of man-hours. And Bill's crew is handling the landscaping, so both of us have been spending a lot of time here, but I didn't think it was an issue. Kira would drop by after school and do her homework here."

"Bill works for you?"

She laughed. "No. He has his landscaping business, Greenscape Gardens."

"Gotcha. I'll be in touch, okay?"

I left Stephanie in her office and hobbled my way back to the car. I wasn't overly concerned that anything terrible had happened to Kira. If she were—heaven forbid—dead, then I'm sure I would have seen her ghost by now because that's what tended to happen whenever I had a case that involved a death. The victim's ghost would appear and either help or hinder me in finding their killer. Then they'd cross over. It was a blessing and a curse.

But there had been no sightings of Kira's ghost. For that, I was thankful. But given her mother's conviction that Kira wouldn't have simply ditched training, something was going on, and that was enough to pique my interest enough to take the case.

Chapter Four

After bandaging my ankle, changing into sweat pants and a T-shirt, and hiding the second box of coffee pods in my closet (because surely my brother wouldn't be bold enough to search there), I lay down on my bed for a brief rest. Okay, nap. I admit I was exhausted. This morning's nerves, coupled with the lack of sleep and decaf coffee, had me running on empty, and Kira deserved me at full strength. I'd just close my eyes for half an hour, and then I'd do what I promised her mother, and that was to find her daughter.

"Mom! Mom! Mom!" The screams coming from downstairs jolted me out of a deep sleep with a certain degree of concern. For one, I was no one's parent, so why someone was tearing through my house screaming for their mother was beyond me. And two, who dared wake me from my slumber? I *needed* this nap! Whoever it was had better have come prepared with coffee. Full strength.

With bleary eyes, I slung my legs over the side of the bed and stood, scratching my butt and tugging my panties from where they'd risen while I'd slept. Heaving a put-upon sigh, I made my way downstairs, adjusting my sweatpants as I went.

"What in God's name is going on?" I stood surveying my downstairs living area that now resembled a war zone. Okay, a war zone was a stretch, but still, I was not pleased with the state of my home. The sofa cushions were on the floor, and the mug I'd left on the coffee table was also on the floor, in pieces. Kitchen cupboard doors stood open, the bin was tipped over, and the contents were very thoroughly rummaged through.

A streak of gray ran past me, screeching, "Mooooooooom!" followed by a streak of black and white making a chittering noise that sounded suspiciously like, "Be my friend, be my friend, be my friend."

"Thor?"

"Save meeeeee!" Thor whizzed past again, a raccoon hot on his heels. Rolling my eyes, I held out my arms. "Come here, then."

Thor about-faced and ran back toward me, leaping into my arms. The raccoon followed suit, only my arms were full, so he attached himself to my thigh instead.

"Ouch! Get off!" I shook my leg, trying to dislodge the critter, but he held fast.

"See," Thor panted, sides heaving as he clung to my shoulder. "He just won't leave me alone."

"I am a she," the raccoon responded, gazing at Thor with adoring eyes. "And I want to be your friend."

"See, Thor?" I grinned. "She just wants to be friends."

Thor shot me a look that suggested he didn't believe it for one second. That was when Ben appeared, caught one look at me with a cat on my chest and raccoon on my leg, and burst into peals of laughter. He laughed long and loud, bent over with his hands on his knees. I waited until he got his mirth under control and pinned him with a glare.

"Was that entirely necessary?" I demanded.

"If you could only see yourself!" He snorted out another laugh.

"Yeah, well, you may laugh, but look what they've done to your house." A low blow because when Ben had been alive, he was one very proud homeowner, a neat freak to be exact. To see his house in disarray was torture, but hey, I wasn't above taking a low shot in retaliation.

Ben sobered immediately and surveyed the damage the two animals had wrought. "Not too bad, I suppose," he mumbled.

"Can I put you down now?" I asked Thor. "I really need coffee, and if you don't want to spend the afternoon licking coffee out of your fur…"

"Yes, once was more than enough, thank you!" Thor huffed, remembering when he'd insisted I hold him while preparing my much needed morning beverage. Needless to say, he'd ended up wearing it.

"I like coffee," the raccoon said. I glanced down at her, hanging off my thigh, my sweatpants slowly creeping southbound.

"Is that right? I'm not sure caffeine is good for you."

"What's caffeine?" She looked up at me, her masked face inquisitive.

I sighed. "Never mind. Look, I'm going to put Thor down. Could you do me a solid and A, not chase him, and B, let go of my leg?"

The raccoon turned her attention to Thor, who returned her look with disdain.

"Will you be my friend?" the raccoon asked.

"No," he promptly replied.

"Thor! That's not nice," I scolded.

"Why? It's the truth."

"I need coffee." Dropping Thor to the ground, I eyed the raccoon, who reluctantly released her grip on my thigh. I tugged my sweats back up before Ben got an eyeful of my underwear. "Do you have a name?" I asked.

"Bandit."

Thor guffawed. "How original."

"Thor," I warned the gray ball of fluff. And then it dawned on me. I was talking to a raccoon. I glanced at Ben, who was still inspecting the havoc the two animals had wreaked on the house. "Ben," I hissed.

He glanced at me. "What?"

"I'm talking to a raccoon."

"Yeah? So?"

"I'm. Talking. To. A. *Raccoon*." I stomped around the counter, wincing at the reminder that my ankle had not miraculously healed since I wrapped it, and into the kitchen, punched the button on the coffee machine with more force than necessary, and grabbed a mug from the overhead cupboard. "How am I talking to a raccoon? Since when can I talk to other animals besides Thor? Oh my God, I'm not turning into Doctor Dolittle, am I? I'm not ready for this."

"Fitz, Fitz." Ben approached and laid a comforting arm around my shoulders, only the icy blast from his touch was far from comforting. "Relax. Maybe it's a phenomenon related to the house?"

I liked his suggestion. It was the only one that made sense. Rubbing at the headache that started to niggle behind my eyes, I waited for my coffee and eyed the two creatures now sitting on my dining room floor. Bandit and Thor.

"Why don't you two go outside?" I suggested, not wanting to deal with any of this until I was suitably caffeinated. Thankfully, my stash of full strength pods helped with that goal considerably.

"I was outside." Thor sniffed. "That's when this terrorist started chasing me."

"What's a terrorist?" Bandit asked.

"You are," Thor snapped. "I don't need another friend. I have Ben. I have Audrey. I don't need you."

I winced at Thor's harsh words, yet Bandit wasn't fazed at all. She bared her teeth at him in what I assumed to be a smile and said, "That's okay. You're *my* friend."

"I don't think you realize how this works," Thor grumbled. "You don't get to decide that I'm your friend."

"Yes, I do."

"Guys! Please. Take this outside, will you?" I couldn't stand to listen to them bickering for another second.

"Fine!" Thor huffed, headbutting the cat door and squeezing through the opening. I frowned. He really was getting round. My eyes fell to his dish with the never-ending supply of kibble. Maybe I needed to stop giving in to his demands of impending starvation. It wasn't the first time I'd had that thought. To be honest, I was putting it off. I didn't relish putting Thor on a diet. Can you imagine the *complaining?*

Bandit followed, hot on Thor's heels. I watched as Thor flicked his tail, catching

Bandit on the side of the face. Bandit didn't flinch. It seemed the raccoon was very much enamored of my cat. I sniggered at the very idea of it.

"Why are you here, anyway?" I asked Ben. I thought for sure he'd still be at the station, following Savannah around.

"She clocked out for the day, and it felt wrong to follow her back to her hotel room."

"She clocked out?" Wow, she wasn't even working full days. Seemed being an internal affairs investigator was a pretty cushy job... providing you didn't mind everyone hating your guts every time you turned up at a station.

"It's past five, Fitz."

I rolled my eyes. "Nice try." Although I did glance at the clock on the wall that was stuck at seven-thirty. Shoulda picked up a battery for it at Nick's Bodega.

"Check your phone," Ben said. With a sinking sensation, I retrieved the phone from my purse, woke up the screen, and let the time displayed in bright numbers sink in. *Five. Thirty.* And that's when it hit me. Kira's case! I'd meant to be working, and instead, I was sleeping. My cup of coffee slipped right through my fingers and hit the floor, where it shattered into a million pieces, along with splashes of my beloved brew soaking the lower half of my sweatpants.

"You okay?" Ben asked, kneeling next to me to begin collecting the shards of broken crockery. Only, of course, he couldn't pick it up. He was incorporeal. But it would be handy if he wasn't. It would be handy if he could actually clean. Running a distracted hand through my hair, I glared at the mess

I'd made, adding to the mess Thor and Bandit had made. My house was trashed, I kept losing track of time, and where the hell was Galloway?

It was Friday. And Friday nights were date night. I should have heard from him by now, but there were no missed calls or messages on my phone. I usually heard from him sometime in the afternoon, making plans for the night ahead.

"Today is apparently lose track of time day," I said absently, firing off a text to Galloway. *"Pizza at mine? Choose your topping. I will be having pineapple,"* I wrote.

"I've got work to do," I said to Ben.

"You sure do. This place is a mess."

"No. Not that type of work. I have a case. Kira Melendez is missing, and I was supposed to be looking into her disappearance this afternoon."

"But you fell asleep."

"I blame whoever switched out my coffee for decaf," I grumbled. "You don't know anything about that, do you?"

"Fitz, you know I can't touch things."

"No, but you can see and hear things. Who was in my house stealing my coffee?"

"Honestly? I didn't see a thing. They must've done it when we were both out."

"Never mind. I'll find out eventually. Right now, I need to find out what I can about Kira—and if she's turned up." Guilt washed over me that I hadn't done the things I'd promised Stephanie Melendez I'd do. If Kira really was missing, I'd lost valuable time.

"How can I help?" Ben asked.

"Can you go to the Melendez house and see if she's home? And if she hasn't turned up yet, can you scout around her room, see if anything strikes you as unusual? You know the drill."

"On it. What's the address?"

"Excellent question." I hadn't even started a file on the case. Limping into the office, I fired up the computer and created a new case file. A quick internet search provided the address, and after reading it over my shoulder, Ben disappeared. Then I started digging into Kira's online presence while simultaneously running her name through my favorite databases. Not that I expected Kira to have a criminal history, but there may be a connection to the Melendez name that could help.

By the time Ben returned, I had a bio on Kira, her best friend Evangeline Blake—

everyone called her Eva—and her boyfriend, Rowan Boyle. If anyone knew anything about Kira's movements and current state of mind, it would be those two.

"She's not home," Ben said. "Her mom and dad are beside themselves."

"I promised I'd call in on them after work. I'll head over now. Anything in her room?"

"Nothing that I could see."

"Okay. While I head to the Melendez's, can you do me a favor and call in to see these two?" I showed him the names of Eva and Rowan. "Best friend. Boyfriend. See if Kira is with either of them."

"Will do."

I shot another text off to Galloway. *"Pizza on hold. Got a case. Will call you when I'm home."*

Changing into a clean pair of jeans, I tossed a jacket over my T-shirt. My swollen ankle and foot dictated the only shoes I'd be wearing today were flip flops—I'd just have to brave the chill in the air as night fell and hope my toes didn't freeze.

Stephanie and Bill Melendez greeted me at my car door. They'd heard a car pull up and had rushed outside, hoping it was Kira. I didn't take the disappointment on their faces personally.

"Shall we go inside?" I suggested. The sun was sliding over the horizon, taking with it not only light but warmth. I shivered and blamed the fact I was cold on the flip flops and my stupid ankle.

"The police won't do anything," Stephanie said, her voice strained. A tear slid past her lashes. "They said if she hasn't turned up by morning to call them."

"And you haven't heard from Kira at all? No text message? Voice mail?"

"We've been calling and texting ever since Coach called Steph," Bill Melendez said. "She's not picking up."

"Her battery may be dead," I pointed out. Or she could be avoiding talking to her parents, but I kept that observation to myself. I studied Bill. Even though I knew Kira obviously had some Hispanic or Latino blood, the name Bill was very white American. But Bill was most definitely Mexican American, from the olive skin to the dark hair to the equally dark eyes.

"I have to ask," I said. "Where does the name Bill come from?"

He snorted out a laugh. "It's a nickname I picked up as a kid. My real name is Raleigh Melendez."

"Can we get on with finding Kira please?" Stephanie cut in, agitation in her voice, her hands clasping and unclasping in front of her.

"Of course. Can you take me to Kira's room?"

"This way."

I followed Stephanie upstairs. I'd been expecting a messy teenager's room, but Kira's room was neat and tidy, albeit the bed hadn't been made so much as the cover tossed over it. I stood looking around then pulled a pair of latex gloves from my back pocket and snapped them on. Stephanie's eyes rounded in horror.

"Just a precaution," I told her. "If Kira has been taken, I don't want to contaminate anything."

Bill cleared the lump of emotion from his throat. "Makes sense." He remained in the doorway, watching. Stephanie crossed to him and sagged into his arms while I began searching Kira's room.

"You're sure Kira didn't take off on her own?" I checked the window for signs of forced entry. Nothing. I scanned the books and papers on the nightstand. Nothing unusual. Same with the desk. Opening the closet door, I scanned the items of clothing hanging up. It wasn't until my eyes landed on the pile of textbooks on the floor of the closet that my heart skipped a beat, and my spidey senses took off.

Crouching, I sorted through the books. Biology, math, English, history, geography.

"What? What is it? What did you find?" Stephanie hurried across the room to crowd in behind me.

"This looks to be all of Kira's textbooks." I swiveled to one side, lost my balance, and hurriedly grabbed the closet door before I landed on my rear.

"Yeah. So?"

"So, you said that Kira had her backpack with her this morning. With, I'd assume, her schoolbooks for the day. Why, then, are they all here?"

"What?" Bill left his post at the door and came to examine the books. "You're right. Everything is here. Including the book she records her track results in." He leaned down and picked up a dog-eared notebook, flicking through the pages. "She's best at one hundred meters but does okay with two hundred and four hundred."

"I'd assume if she'd intended to go to training today, she'd have taken that?" I cocked my head toward the book in his hands.

"Of course. Steph, is her training gear in there?"

I moved out of the way while Stephanie went through Kira's closet. Stuffed at the back in a plastic bag were Kira's running shorts, top, and shoes.

Stephanie held it with a stunned look on her face. "I can't... I just..." she stammered. She was in shock. Full of disbelief that her daughter's disappearance was intentional. At least at first glance.

"She wouldn't ditch training," Bill protested.

I raised a brow. Yet clearly, she had. Bill caught my look and deflated before my eyes, his shoulders rounding and hunching in, his chin sinking to his chest. That's when I realized he was crying.

"Oh. Uh." I patted his arm in an awkward gesture, unsure how to comfort the man.

Stephanie came to my rescue. "Oh, honey." Dropping the plastic bag, she enveloped her husband in a warm hug.

I sidled away, back toward Kira's desk. I pulled out the chair and sat down, keen to get the weight off my ankle. Nothing on the desk was amiss, and it really did look like Kira had run away and not been taken, but there had to be a clue here somewhere about where she'd gone.

The desk had two drawers, and I slid open the top one, peering inside to find a bunch of papers that looked like she'd just swept her arm across the desk and shoved them all into the drawer. I pulled them out and sifted through them. There was a flyer for the Ivelisse Day Spa that looked like it had been screwed into a ball and then smoothed out again. A training timetable. A bunch of take-out menus. Odd for a teenager obsessed with track and field and her eye on the Olympics to have take-out menus. I assumed she followed a fairly strict diet. I wasn't sure what that meant, if anything.

Nothing leaped out at me as unusual aside from the menus. I was about to put it all back when I saw I'd missed a postcard at the bottom of the drawer. I held it up. The picture was of a gorgeous house, not too dissimilar from the one Stephanie had renovated for her day spa. Flipping it over, I narrowed my eyes at what was printed on the back. Divine Delights Spa and Resort. The address was the next town over.

"Was Kira scouting out the competition for you?" I asked, waving the postcard.

"What?" Stephanie sniffed and wiped her fingers under her eyes then plucked the postcard from my grasp. "Oh, this is Holly Wilson's place."

"A friend of yours?"

"I guess you could say we have a friendly rivalry." Stephanie nodded. "I visited all the local spas and beauty retreats as part of my research in renovating Ivelisse."

"Any idea why Kira would have kept this? There's no other pamphlets or advertising material for the other places."

Stephanie shrugged. "It probably got caught up in those takeout menus of hers. Kira has a bit of an obsession with them. She adheres to a strict diet—for training purposes—but likes to collect the menus and... dream, I guess."

I couldn't imagine being that disciplined at fifteen not to eat junk food. Heck, I wasn't that disciplined now! But it explained the collection of menus, and I figured it would have been easy enough for Kira to accidentally scoop up the postcard when she took the menus that most likely turned up in the junk mail.

Tossing the postcard back, I opened the second drawer. More of the same. A bunch of graded papers, old magazines. From the depths of the drawer, I pulled out a journal. *Bingo*. I flipped through the pages briefly before sliding it into my purse. I'd examine it in more detail at home.

I stood and addressed the Melendezes, huddled together in a world of grief and pain. My heart ached for them, it truly did, but what we were looking at here was a runaway, which, in my book, was better than if Kira had been taken. It took away that element of immediate danger.

"Is there anywhere you'd think Kira
would go?"

Stephanie sniffed and wiped her tears away.
"Besides the track? I've already called her
best friend, Eva. And Rowan. They say they
haven't seen her."

"I have someone checking them out now." If
Kira didn't want her parents to know where
she was, she'd have sworn her friends to
secrecy. But Ben was my secret weapon.
He'd know for sure if Kira was hiding out
with Eva or Rowan.

Adjusting the shoulder strap of my purse, I
limped toward the door. "Try not to worry. I'll
find her. Let me know if you hear from her,
okay?"

Trekking down the stairs with a shot ankle
was no fun, and I was sorely tempted to ride
the banister down, but knowing my luck, I'd
topple over the side and hurt myself even

worse. I could hear Stephanie and Bill Melendez's softly muted voices as they discussed their runaway daughter. After I closed the door behind me, I stood for a moment in the twilight on their front porch and wondered... what was so bad that Kira had run away?

Chapter Five

"All we know is that she wasn't in school today," I said to Ben when I walked in the front door. The house was still a mess, but it would have to wait. A missing teenager was still a missing teenager, and even if she *had* run away, it didn't mean bad things couldn't happen. Making myself yet another coffee—hopefully, this one I'd actually get to consume—I headed into my office. There was no sign of Thor or Bandit, and I wasn't sure if that was a good thing or a bad thing.

"She wasn't at Evangeline's or Rowan's." Ben said. "But I did find out something interesting."

"Oh?"

"The two of them were playing a dedicated game of tonsil hockey."

I swiveled my chair to face Ben. "Really? Eva and Rowan were hooking up?"

"Uh-huh." He nodded. "But I searched both their places. Kira is definitely not hiding out with either of them."

"Where would she go?" It was a rhetorical question. Had Kira found out her boyfriend was cheating on her with her best friend? That kind of betrayal was huge. Devastating. "Oh! I have Kira's journal." I hurried out to the living room where I'd left my purse and retrieved the diary.

"Kids still do that?"

"Lots of people keep diaries or journals. It's very cathartic."

"Do you?"

I shook my head. "No. But Laura does." My sister had always scribbled in her journal late at night under the covers when we were kids. And while she didn't need to hide under the covers these days, I knew she still kept a journal because she'd told me. It helped keep her head straight, she'd said. Write out the things that were bothering her, stressing her. It took some of their power away.

"Did Kira have a laptop or computer in her room?"

I paused. "I didn't see one." Which was odd. I made a mental note to ask her parents about a laptop. Settling back into my chair, I began reading Kira's journal. One thing was apparent. She really was dedicated to her sport. She chastised herself for bad times or a slip in her diet, scolded herself to do better.

"Oh. Here's something," I glanced at Ben, who was sitting on the desk next to me. I began to read from the journal. "I'm telling him today. He's leaving for college soon anyway. It'll be easier to break things off now rather than drag out a long-distance relationship that's doomed to fail. I feel kinda bad that I'm excited about the extra time I'll have to devote to training. Coach warned me having a boyfriend was a bad idea, but I'm not going to tell him he was right."

"Wait. So, Kira broke up with Rowan?" Ben asked.

"Looks that way."

"When was that entry dated?"

"Couple of days ago." But Kira's parents didn't know about the breakup, or they'd have told me. "So, the question is, did she go through with it? Did she break up with Rowan?"

"You're going to have to go and talk with him," Ben said.

"I will. Just as soon as I finish my coffee." Leaning back in my chair, I propped my foot up on the desk and cradled my cup in one hand, the journal in the other.

"You should get a doctor to take a look at that." Ben nodded at my ankle.

"Nah. Just a sprain." I was not a fan of doctors or hospitals. Purely because I'd had way too many visits for way too many various injuries over the years that now I'd do anything to avoid a trip to emergency. Like walking on a broken ankle. Not that I thought it was broken. But I'd done some muscle damage for sure.

"You know what strikes me as odd?" I asked, changing the subject.

"What?"

"From what I'm reading in her journal and what her parents have said, Kira is a dedicated athlete. Like, I mean, obsessive. She is laser-focused on her goals and is serious about making the Olympic team." I only wish I had half of that focus, grit, and determination.

"So why run away?"

I pointed my cup at him. "That's it exactly. What's the catalyst? What monumental event happened that made her decide to leave?"

"Well, it's not the boyfriend. She'd already dumped him or was intending to. Something with her best friend?"

I sighed, drained my cup, and lowered my foot to the floor. "One way to find out. Where were Eva and Rowan hanging out?"

"His place."

* * *

"I swear, Miss Fitzgerald, I don't know where she is," Rowan Boyle pleaded that I believe him. Just so happens, I did. But his mom didn't seem too happy that I was on her doorstep questioning her son over a missing girl.

"Had the two of you broken up?"

A hint of red dusted across his cheekbones, and his eyes refused to meet mine. Instead, he seemed intent on examining my feet, which were probably blue due to the cold, considering I was out in flip flops. Winter may have ended, but it was still cold. Spring hadn't quite sprung yet.

"Rowan, answer the woman so we can get this settled." His mom clipped him over the back of the head, and I flinched. I could see why Rowan was keen to move away for college.

"Mrs. Boyle?" I used my most authoritative voice. "This might go quicker if I could speak with Rowan alone. I assure you, he's not in trouble." Not unless he'd done something to Kira. Like, pressure her into sex. Date rape was still a thing, sadly, and if it turned out Rowan had used his physical size and strength to force Kira into doing something she didn't want to do? Then yeah, he was in big trouble, and I'd make it my priority that he paid the price.

"Fine. You have five minutes, and then I want you off my property. He has a game in the morning and needs his sleep."

"Thank you."

The front door slammed behind her, and I winced as the windows rattled. I took a couple of steps backward. "Come away from the house." I beckoned him to follow. "Where your mom won't overhear." I had no doubt she was inside the living room right now with her ear pressed against the window.

Rowan cast a glance over his shoulder then quickly followed. "Look, I swear I don't know where Kira is."

"Did she break up with you?" I repeated my question.

"Yes," he mumbled.

"Was that before you hooked up with her best friend or after?"

Rowan blanched, the color leaving his face before returning in a veritable flood of red. "During," he choked.

"Did she know?"

He shook his head. "The thing with Eva... just... happened. Like, I've always liked her in a friendly way. The three of us spent time together, so I got to know her pretty well."

"Were you and Kira having sex?"

He quickly shook his head, and I scoffed. "Come on, Rowan. You're a jock. While you may not be the captain of the football team, you're a very popular player, and I'm sure you have a certain reputation to uphold."

"Coach would kill me if I laid a hand on Kira in that way!"

"Coach? What does he have to do with this?"

"He's grooming Kira for the Olympics. He thinks she could be his ticket to bigger things. He warned me not to interfere with her training program in any way, and that included sleeping with her. He said he'd know if I did, and he'd drop me from the football team. I believed him. The two of them are very close."

I digested that and knew I'd circle around to ponder it some more later, but right now, I needed to focus my attention on Rowan. "So, what happened? Kira is off-limits. Why not dump her? You're eighteen. No need for you to be celibate just because Coach says so."

"I didn't dump her because I really liked her, and sex is just sex. I'm not that guy that forces a girl to put out or he'll dump her. Kira has this..." He raised his eyes to the night sky, searching for the words. "She's driven. I really admire that in her. And yeah, it's true, hanging out with her was mostly about track, football, and training, but I liked that she got it. She got me and what the game means to me. Most girls don't. They want to hang with a jock but then get resentful that I have to train and that the game comes before them. Kira wasn't like that."

"And yet, Eva."

His face fell. "Yeah. I feel bad about that."

"But not bad enough to stop seeing her. Are you and Eva sleeping together?" Not that it mattered. I was just curious.

"She's sixteen."

"I'll take that as a yes." I sighed. Teenagers and hormones. "Could it be that Eva developed a conscience and told Kira about the two of you?"

He blinked in surprise. "She'd have told me." But I could see on his face that he wasn't quite sure if that were true.

"If Kira found out, what do you think she'd do?"

"She'd probably chew me out about it," he mumbled. "Call me a loser who was thinking with his wiener."

"That's it? She wouldn't do anything… drastic?"

He shrugged. "Doubtful. I told you. There really is only one thing that is important to Kira, and that's her potential career as a professional athlete. Sure, she'd be angry at me. And Eva. Maybe not talk to us for a while."

"Okay, well, thanks for your time, Rowan." I handed him my business card. "If you hear from Kira, please contact me. It's important."

He nodded. "I will."

"Oh, and good luck with the game tomorrow."

After leaving the Boyles' house, I headed toward the Blakes' house, keen to hear Eva's version of events. On the way, I called Galloway, leaving a voicemail when he didn't pick up. "Hey babe, just me. Call me when you get the chance."

Ben appeared in the passenger seat, startling the ever-loving bejeezus out of me so that I swerved and nearly ran the car off the road. "Ben!" I gasped, my heart thundering in my chest. "Don't do that! And how did you do that?"

"Do what?"

"Materialize in a moving vehicle."

"I'm a ghost, Fitz. I can do what I want."

"But how does that work?"

"Dunno. I just think about where I want to be, and I'm there."

"Like teleporting." I nodded, flexed my fingers on the wheel, and calmed my breath.

"Pretty much. Sorry I missed your chat with Rowan. How did it go?"

"I don't think anything happened between him and Kira. I had a hunch that maybe he'd forced her into something... but he says he didn't, and I believe him."

"You sure?"

"As sure as I can be. Maybe he has me fooled, who knows. But I'm going to talk with Eva now, see what she has to say for herself. I know you boys have your bro code, but us girls have the sisterhood, and Eva has let it down by fooling around with her best friend's guy."

"What did Rowan say about that?"

"That it happened before he and Kira broke up. And after. And that he and Kira didn't have sex. Coach's orders."

"Say what?"

I glanced at Ben out the corner of my eye. "Right? I found that odd too. Don't worry, Coach is on my list."

"Hang on a second, you're going to Eva's now? She wasn't at Rowan's?"

"Nope. He was alone. Well, along with his mom, and she wasn't too happy to have me questioning her boy."

"Weird. Not even nine o'clock on a Friday night, and he's home alone? Where did Eva go?"

"Maybe they're heading out later? I remember as a teenager, we used to get loaded at home and then sneak out, already half cut." Gah, if Mom only knew the trouble

I used to get into when I was younger, she'd have a conniption.

Ben snorted. "I remember. I also remember you puking all over my shoes."

"You were the perfect gentleman, holding my hair back."

"That was a rocking party, though, wasn't it?" He grinned. My mind flashed back to the summer when I was seventeen. Jordan Rigby held the wildest party the kids of Firefly Bay High had ever seen. Zero parental supervision, a keg, and a bottle of Malibu. To this day, I couldn't stand the smell of the stuff.

"It sure was. You had to abandon your date to bring me home."

"Don't worry, it earned me brownie points." He grinned.

I held up my hand in a classic stop signal. "Don't tell me. I don't want to know."

After pulling up in front of Evangeline Blake's house, I killed the engine then sat in the dark looking at the house. Nothing special about it. Yet every light was ablaze. The place was lit up like a Christmas tree.

"That's not good for the electricity bill," I muttered, sliding out of the car and hobbling to the front door. My ankle was not at all pleased with the extra walking I was putting it through this evening. Not to worry, after speaking with Eva, I planned on calling in on Coach and then heading home, where I'd lay on the sofa with a bag of peas on the protesting joint.

A young boy around ten years old opened the door when I knocked.

"Oh, hi." I smiled. "Is Eva home?"

"Eva!" the kid yelled. "Some lady here to see you!"

"Who is it?" The voice came from somewhere deep within the house.

"Dunno." And then he slammed the door in my face.

I turned my head to look at Ben. "Don't worry," he said, "I'm already on it." He stepped through the door.

A solid minute passed before the door opened once more, and I assumed Evangeline Blake stood before me. For one, she looked Kira's age, and two, she looked eerily similar to Kira. Long dark brown hair, olive skin, only instead of blue eyes, Evangeline's were brown.

"Yes?"

"Hi Eva, I'm Audrey Fitzgerald, a private investigator. You may have heard that your friend, Kira Melendez, is missing?"

Eva shifted weight from one foot to the other, her hip jutting out. "I heard." I couldn't make out if it was concern in her voice or disdain.

"Have you seen or heard from Kira today?" I prompted.

"Nope."

I sighed. "Okay, look. I've just come from Rowan's house, and I know all about you and him. I also know that you were seeing him while he was still dating Kira, so let's cut the bull, huh?"

Her face crumpled, and her eyes welled with tears. She blinked, and big fat drops overflowed to run down her cheeks.

"We never meant to hurt her," Eva whispered, wiping her face. "We both love her."

"Right. So... did she know? About the two of you?"

Eva shook her head. "It got... messy." She sniffed. "It was after track a couple of weeks back. Kira ditched early. She didn't want to grab a pizza with us because, you know, her diet. But Rowan was in the mood to celebrate. He'd had a good training session. Coach was pleased, so he and I grabbed a pizza and then...we didn't plan it. One thing led to another."

Her anguish was real. My heart went out to her. Not that I condoned cheating. Still, I remembered teenage hormones all too well and some of the rather idiotic decisions I'd made in my youth.

I patted her on the shoulder. "I get it."

Eva sniffed loudly, and I dug in my purse for a tissue, waiting while she blew her nose.

"We were trying to decide what to do. What it meant. Rowan and I discovered we liked each other—more than friends."

"So, he was building up to ending it with Kira?"

"He didn't want to hurt her."

A bit late for that, but I kept my mouth shut. "But then Kira got in first. What prompted that, do you think? Did she know about the two of you?"

Eva shook her head. "Kira would have given us both hell over it if she'd known. I think she just wanted to focus more on her training. Plus, she'd been talking a bit about how Rowan would be going away for college soon, and I don't think she was interested in maintaining a long-distance relationship."

That echoed exactly what Kira had written in her journal.

Ben reappeared, standing behind Eva. "Nothing to report," he said. "Looks like the Blakes have a dozen kids. And still no sign of Kira. She's not hiding out here."

"If Kira was upset over something, where would she go?" I asked Eva.

"The track. She'd run." Eva looked at me for a moment, chewing her lip. "You don't think something happened to her, do you? Something bad?"

"I hope not, but it's my job to find out." I handed Eva my card. "If you hear from her, please call. Even if she asks you not to. There's a time to protect your friends and a time to help them. Kira needs your help."

Eva took the card with trembling fingers and bloodshot eyes. "I'll call. I promise. Please find her."

Chapter Six

It was Friday night before a big game, and Coach was wasted. I'd almost keeled over when the stench of alcohol emanating from him reached my nose. I coughed to cover my reaction and turned my head to suck in a breath of fresh air.

"Coach Cox?"

Lowell Cox was mid-fifties, balding, and overweight. He was also roaring drunk, his green eyes dull as he frowned at me. "Wh're you?" he slurred.

"Audrey Fitzgerald, private investigator. I'm looking into the disappearance of Kira Melendez."

"My star pupil!" he wailed dramatically, throwing his arms up in the air and almost toppling over at the movement. He made a mad grab for the door jamb while I stepped closer than I liked and took his arm in a firm grip.

"How about we get you inside, hmm?" I suggested, grabbing his arm.

"She wouldn't miss training, y'know," he continued. "Not my Kira. Never met a kid like 'er."

I wrangled him through the door and toward a worn armchair with tufts of stuffing poking out the back. Coach fell into it.

"What do you think happened?" I asked.

"Hmmm?"

"To Kira? Where is she?"

"I don't know. But she wouldn't miss training. Not ever." He swung his arm out, clipped an empty beer bottle on the table next to him, and sent it flying. I watched as it hit the floor and rolled under the sofa. I had an uncomfortable feeling, standing in Coach's living room, that Coach was one of those people who'd peaked early in life, and then everything had been downhill ever since. Beer cans and empty liquor bottles littered almost every available surface, side-by-side with trophies from years of old.

"You used to play?" I asked, bending to read the name engraved on one of the trophies. Sure enough, Lowell Cox, footballer of the year, nineteen eighty-six.

"Headed for the big leagues until injury took me out."

This was the room of a lonely man, and it made me inexplicably sad.

"Tell me about Kira." I eyed the sofa and considered sitting, but I couldn't be one hundred percent sure what the stains were. Beer or...

"Best student eva," he slurred.

"Yeah, I got that. You're probably the one person she spent the most time with. Tell me about her. What does she like? Dislike?"

"She dumped Boyle." Coach wiped his nose on his sleeve. "Best move she ever made. Told her not to get involved with him. No time for boys when you're training."

"I know all about Rowan Boyle," I assured him. Ben, who'd disappeared to search the house for any sign of Kira, reappeared. He shook his head. Kira wasn't here, and given the state of Coach, I was glad.

"But what else was going on with her? What did she talk about? Did she seem upset?" I paused for a moment, giving Coach time to answer. When he didn't, I peered at him in the dim light. I'd be blowed if he hadn't dozed off. I nudged his foot, and he jerked awake.

"Who're you?" he demanded, eyeing me suspiciously.

I rolled my eyes. "I'm a private investigator hired to find Kira Melendez."

"My star pupil!"

"Yes. We've been over that. You were telling me what the two of you used to talk about."

He waved an arm around, narrowly missing another empty bottle. I leaned forward and moved it out of reach.

"You know. Usual stuff."

"Like what?"

"Home stuff." He crossed his arms over his chest, his chin lowering.

I nudged his foot again. "Don't go to sleep. Not yet. It's important we find Kira."

"Might wanna start with the parents," he mumbled. "Kids used to tease Kira that Bill ain't her dad."

"What?" I blinked, glanced at Ben, who shrugged, then turned my attention back to Coach. "Why did they say that?"

"Something about a Latino with blue eyes."

"Um. Her mother has blue eyes," I pointed out.

Coach raised a hand and made a motion to wave me away. "Kira was mad at her dad," he said.

"Do you know why?"

Coach sat up straighter at that and seemed alert for the first time. "Kira got an offer from an ex-professional footballer to be her manager. For the Olympics. Michael Campbell was a gridiron superstar, best midfielder I have ever seen. Retired due to injury, but he manages his own team now. Anyways, Bill said no."

"Any idea why?" Seemed like a heck of an opportunity for an up-and-coming Olympic hopeful to have a manager helping her out. I wasn't much into football, but the name Michael Campbell rang a bell.

"Who would say no to Mikey Campbell managing their daughter's athletic career?" Ben piped up. "That guy is loaded. He doesn't just manage his team. He owns them. And get this—he comes from Firefly Bay. He was signed at seventeen, retired from football at thirty-five, and made an absolute fortune in between. He must be, oh, early forties now."

I glanced back at Coach, but his chin was on his chest, and his snores grew louder with each breath. I sighed. "Well, she's not here, but we learned something new. All is not as it seems at the Melendez house."

"I'd be interested in why Bill said no to the manager offer." Ben nodded, following me out the front door that I dutifully locked behind me. I suspected Coach fell asleep, drunk in his chair, most nights.

"Right?" I wondered that too. "Do you think maybe Kira ditched school and training to go see this Michael Campbell guy? He wants to be her manager, and her dad said no. I can't imagine Kira would be happy about that. Maybe she's gone to see him and ask him to be her manager without her parents knowing?"

"That's a sticky legal minefield." Ben frowned.

"I know. But Kira is a headstrong teenager who has one goal in life. Make the Olympics. Something tells me she'll do anything to make that goal a reality. Even ditching town to go see Campbell. Where is he, anyway? The city?"

"Yeah. Has offices in a highrise right in the middle of the CBD. Lives in a penthouse in the same building."

"Heck of a commute," I snorted, climbing into my car. I tossed my purse onto the passenger seat and then rummaged for my phone. I checked for messages—there were none—then dialed Galloway, throwing the phone into the cup holder and letting the call connect via the car's Bluetooth. I started the engine and checked for traffic before pulling away from the curb.

"You've reached Detective Kade Galloway. Leave a message." His voicemail kicked in.

"Hey. It's me. I guess you've picked up a case. Sooooo. I'm heading home now if you want to drop by when you're done? If not, that's cool, but give me a call to let me know you're okay. Okay? Love you." I disconnected the call and turned on the radio.

"You're not worried?" Ben asked.

I glanced at him. "About?"

"Galloway."

"Why would I be worried about Galloway?" I frowned.

"Well, you haven't heard from him since this morning."

"You think something's happened to him?" That got my heart rate kicking up a notch.

"But no. If something had happened, someone would have told me." My heart settled back into its normal rhythm.

"No, not that something happened to him."

"Ben, what are you getting at?"

"I can't believe you're this naive," he mumbled, turning from facing me to facing the windshield.

"What are you even talking about? Just spit it out. You clearly want to say something."

"Galloway's ex is in town. And now he's not taking your calls. Hello?"

I barked out a laugh. "Are you serious? You think he's ditched me for Savannah?" I didn't believe it for a second.

"It's possible." He crossed his arms over his chest as if affronted that I didn't think the same thing.

"Savannah is a lovely person. Galloway is a decent guy. They had a thing, and it didn't work out. End of story. Just because they used to date doesn't mean they can't work together and keep things professional."

"How are you so calm about this?"

"Why are you so worked up about it? Look, Ben, it's sweet that you're worried about my relationship with Kade, but seriously, relax. I trust him. He can be friends with other women. I'm honestly not that insecure."

"Maybe you should be. Maybe you shouldn't be so trusting."

I arched a brow. Well, tried to. Both brows shot up into my hairline, giving me a startled look rather than the cool and debonair questioning look I was going for. "I thought Kade was your friend," I pointed out.

"He is."

"But you don't trust him?" Where was this even coming from? "Oh! I get it." I snapped my fingers and pointed at him. "You were cheated on. One of your girlfriends got back with an ex."

He cleared his throat and turned his attention to the side window, so I couldn't see his face.

"Okay. To humor you, why don't you go check up on them? See what Savannah and Galloway are up to. You said Savannah had left the station at five. Go see where she is now and what she's doing."

"Really?" He turned to face me, eyes wide.

"Really. Go spy on my boyfriend if it will make you feel better, but for the record, I do not think they are doing anything clandestine other than police work."

He nodded and disappeared.

I meant what I'd said. I had no issues with Savannah being in town. Did I envy her? Hells yeah. In the way that every woman envies a drop-dead gorgeous woman. I wished I had her long silky hair. I wished I was as tall and elegant. But I wasn't jealous. In fact, once we'd gotten through the formalities of my deposition this morning, we'd had a laugh and a chat, and I could see Savannah and myself becoming friends.

I chewed on my lip as I pulled into my driveway. It was odd that Galloway hadn't at least sent me a quick text in response to my calls, though. That wasn't like him, but I figured he had good reason. Maybe he was on a stakeout or something. Maybe his phone was dead. Doubtful, though. I was the one who constantly had phone issues. But either way, I wasn't too concerned. There'd be a reasonable explanation. And in the meantime, I had a throbbing ankle that demanded I get my weight off it and apply some ice.

Rolling into the garage, I killed the engine and climbed out the driver's side, coming around to the passenger side to grab my purse. I picked up my phone from the cup holder, slid it into my pocket, and was just straightening when a cloth clamped over my mouth.

"Urgh," I mumbled through the gag, twisting and wriggling, trying to break the iron grip of whoever had me pinned between my car and their body. The cloth over my mouth smelled disgusting. And chemically. And it was unavoidable to not breathe it in since it was clamped over my mouth and nose. The world dipped and swayed, I felt dizzy and sweaty and downright odd, my limbs turned to sand, and no matter what I did, I couldn't move them, couldn't get them to work right. Then I passed out.

Chapter Seven

Waking up in the trunk of a car was not my usual Friday night activity. Nor what I would call a good time. The vehicle in question was traveling at speed, and without the benefit of an upholstered seat, I felt every little bump, my body bouncing and jarring as we sped along what had to be an unsealed road.

It was dark, so dark I couldn't see my hand in front of my face. I blinked a few times, hoping my eyes would adjust, but the darkness was all-consuming, with no illumination from dashboard lights back here. I felt around with my hands, making a mental note that it was interesting I wasn't bound. That told me my captor didn't have far to travel and thought I'd remain unconscious for the duration. He thought wrong.

The trunk was empty, save for me. My purse hadn't joined me, but as I lay there trying not to hyperventilate at my predicament, I remembered my phone. I'd slid it into my pocket rather than dropping it into my purse. I reached for it and almost yelped with joy when I felt the familiar shape outlined in denim. Sliding it out of my pocket, I opened the flashlight app, blinding myself when it came on.

Holding the light, I examined the trunk, knowing I didn't have much time. I needed something, anything, to use as a weapon. I'd have the element of surprise but only briefly. Only... there was literally nothing in the trunk. No jack. No tools. Nothing. Leaving the flashlight on, I dialed Galloway. While the call was connecting, I laid the phone down and started to tug at the trunk's lining, trying to hook my fingers in behind the hard plastic casing separating the car's interior from the exterior. I remembered seeing it in a movie once. If you were ever trapped in a trunk, bust out a taillight. Only the taillights were sealed off. I had to get to them first.

I heard the call connect. Galloway's voicemail sounded unbelievably loud in the confined space. I leaned down to the phone while continuing to attempt to get to the taillight and whispered, "Galloway. I'm in some dude's trunk. I've been kidnapped. This isn't a joke. I know it sounds like a joke, and you probably think I'm pulling some sort of stunt to get your attention, but believe me, I'm not. This is rinky-dink real, and I think I need help for this one."

With no guarantees he'd even check his voicemail anytime soon or listen to the three messages I'd already left him, I hung up and dialed the police station.

"Firefly Bay Police Department," a female voice answered.

"This is Audrey Fitzgerald," I whispered. "I've been kidnapped. I'm in the trunk of a car. I don't know where we're headed, but can you trace my phone or something?"

"Sorry, I didn't catch that. Can you speak up?"

I repeated myself, careful not to speak too loudly in case whoever was driving heard me. I wanted him to think I was still out cold. If he knew I was awake, he'd be ready for me. I had one shot at freedom, and that involved taking him by surprise.

I had my suspicions about who my captor was, for while the hand over my mouth and the arm around my chest had been strong, the belly at my back had been big and soft. A belly much like the one Ian Mills sported. And out of all the people who'd want me gone, Mills was top of the list. Actually, there wasn't a list. I didn't think anyone else in Firefly Bay had a beef with me, just Mills. So, yeah. He was my one and only suspect. And while he'd had the upper hand in drugging me, the guy was still an idiot. For one, he'd miscalculated how long I'd be out, and two, he'd failed to remove my phone.

"I'm sorry," the voice on the end of the line said. "You are going to have to speak up.

There's some sort of interference on the line." The interference was the sound of tires on the road, but I dared not speak louder in case Mills heard me. I stopped tugging at the lining over the taillight and picked up the phone, bringing the speaker right up to my mouth.

"Audrey Fitzgerald," I hissed. "Kidnapped. In the trunk of a car."

"Audrey?"

"Yes! Can't talk. I'm in trouble. Can you trace this call? Or my phone?"

I could hear a commotion in the background, the sound of voices conferring, then a different voice came down the line. One I recognized.

"Audrey, this is Sergeant Young. Is it correct that you're reporting a kidnapping?"

"Yes. Mine. I was drugged and tossed in the trunk of a car. We're still moving. I don't know what direction we're headed. I'm trying to bust out a taillight."

"Smart move," Sergeant Addison Young replied, and I could picture her nodding in my mind's eye. "Keep the line open. We're on it."

I really, really hoped so. The car turned a corner, and I slid across the floor, bumping my head. I stifled my groan. Unconscious people did not groan. Wriggling back to my initial position, I got back to the taillight situation, finally getting my fingers beneath the lining and ripping it back. I was bathed in sweat by the time I'd managed to pull enough away to get my hand through. Gritting my teeth, I sucked in a breath, curled my hand into a fist, and punched.

Pain ricocheted up my arm. I was pretty sure I'd just cut myself on the lining as my flesh scraped against it, and I'd possibly broken some fingers as I punched through the plastic, but it was worth it. I'd knocked out the taillight and could feel the cold night air on my skin. What I hadn't factored in was that Mills would hear the breaking plastic. Or maybe he'd felt the car shudder as I'd punched through. Either way, the car slowed.

"Darn, darn, darn," I whispered, maneuvering my arm out of the taillight while doing my best not to scratch myself up any further. Although at least I'd be leaving DNA behind. A small comfort because now I was second-guessing myself. What if this wasn't Mills? What if my unknown assailant had a gun? They could shoot me without even opening the trunk. But if they'd wanted to shoot me, they would have done it already. Why kidnap me?

Maneuvering myself so my head was facing the back seat, I lay on my back, my legs curled up to my chest, ready to kangaroo kick whoever popped the lid on the trunk. I concentrated on my breathing as the car slowed to a halt, the tires crunching on gravel.

Picking up the phone, I whispered, "I hope you guys are hearing this," and held it up, flashlight ready to blind whoever popped the trunk. The car stopped. I felt the vibration shift as the transmission was moved into park then heard the slamming of the door.

"What the heck?" A male voice. Could be Mills. Sounded like Mills, but I was hyper-aware that it could be wishful thinking on my part. Then the trunk popped open. My legs shot out, but my captor moved to the side, and I failed to connect. Then a spray of moisture hit me in the face, and my eyeballs caught on fire.

"Argh!" I screamed, dropping the phone. "You pepper sprayed me?" With my legs already hanging over the edge of the now open trunk, I heaved myself out altogether and fell to my hands and knees on the road. Through the searing pain in my eyes, I felt the ground beneath me. Not asphalt. We were on a gravel road, which meant we could be anywhere.

I heard a put-upon sigh, then Mills grabbed a fistful of my hair and pulled my head back. I screamed some more. More to kick up a fuss and make a lot of noise just in case there was someone in the vicinity who might hear.

"Shut up. You want water to wash out your eyes or not?"

I quit screaming. I'd give my left ovary to wash my face right now.

The grip on my hair was released. "Here." Something hard bounced off the side of my head and fell to the ground. It made a sloshing noise so I figured it was a bottle of water and madly began pawing the ground for it. My fingers eventually closed around the plastic and I fumbled with the lid until I eventually got it open. Tipping my head back I poured water over my face. Sweet, blissful, cooling water. I blinked, trying to wash out the pepper spray dissolving my eyeballs, and through my blurry vision, I could just make out the silhouette of Officer Ian Mills looming over me.

I sat on the ground, dripping wet, and did my best to eyeball him. Seems my attempted intimidation failed to deliver because he kicked me and growled, "Get up."

Struggling to my feet, I looked around for my phone. "What do you want, Mills?" I asked overly loudly, hoping the line with the Firefly Bay PD was still open.

"Looking for this?"

I glanced up. In his hand was my phone. He examined the screen, hit the disconnect button, and then hurled the phone into the woods.

"You know you can just take the sim card out, right?" I grumbled. "I lose more phones in this line of work."

"Get back in the trunk," he ordered.

"I'd rather not." I mean, why stop and open the trunk if you didn't want me out of the trunk? Silly man. And now that I was out, I had no intention of getting back in. "What's your game plan here, Mills? If you wanted to stop me from testifying, you're too late. I already gave my deposition." He looked surprised at that, and I pounced. "Oooh. Did you get some bad intel? Did someone tell you I hadn't been interviewed by internal affairs yet?" I narrowed my eyes, trying to read his expression, but it was dark out here, the glow from the taillights our only illumination, and my vision was dodgy at best. "Was it Sergeant Clements?"

"Get. In. The. Trunk." He grabbed my arm and shoved me toward the car. Seems Mills had forgotten our last run in, that I wasn't above fighting dirty, because there was no way I was meekly going to get back in that vehicle. This was my one shot at freedom. I'd had a chance to recon the area—a secluded dirt road surrounded by woods on both sides. Easy enough to hide in. He'd opened the trunk without a flashlight or gun. But he'd had pepper spray, and my still stinging eyes and soaking wet T-shirt were testament to what an effective weapon it was. Only it was an up-close and personal one.

Amongst the pushing and shoving, he managed to get behind me and wrap his arms around my chest, squeezing and lifting at the same time. My feet left the ground, but as he went to toss me in the trunk, they shot out, and I wedged them against the lower opening and braced myself. He grunted, I wheezed for breath.

"You are such a pain in my—" he began, but I interrupted his cussing with a headbutt. The back of my skull connected with his nose. The crunch was gross but oddly satisfying and had the desired effect. His grip loosened, and I wriggled free. His hands shot out, trying to grab me, but I darted to the side and slammed the trunk closed. Only his hands were in the way, and I may have smiled when I closed the trunk on them. He bellowed. I ran.

My ankle was not at all impressed with this new turn of events as I lunged off the track and into the woods. I was immediately enveloped in darkness, the tall trees blocking not only the small amount of illumination from the moon but the glow of the car lights too. I kept going, shoving my way through the undergrowth, bumping into trees, and feeling my way around them as I blindly stumbled deeper and deeper into the woods.

Eventually, I stopped, my ankle throbbing. I leaned back against a tree trunk and tried to listen for sounds of Mills following me, but it was hard to hear anything over my own rasping breath and thundering heartbeat. Sucking in a deep breath, I held it and listened. Nothing. No crunching twigs or leaves. Releasing the breath, I slid down the trunk to sit on the ground, stretching my legs out in front of me.

"Now what, Fitz?" I whispered to myself. I had no idea where I was, how far away civilization was. And it was pitch black, I couldn't see a thing. The wind whistled through the treetops, and I shivered. My wet T-shirt clung to my skin, the cold seeping deeper, so deep I could feel it in my bones.

Shrugging out of my jacket, I pulled my T-shirt over my head then put my jacket back on, zipping it all the way to my chin. At least the jacket was dry. It would keep me warm enough for now. While I sat and pondered my current predicament, I wrapped the wet T-shirt around my ankle—may as well make use of the unexpected cold compress while I came up with an escape plan.

It's entirely possible I drifted off to sleep, for the next thing I knew, there was a light shining in my eyes and a voice yelling, "Found her!"

"Argh!" I yelled, grabbing a handful of leaves and forest debris from beside me and tossing it at my captor. The leaves fluttered to the ground a good two feet short of their target. I was feeling around for something more substantial, like a rock, when he said, "Audrey, relax. It's Noah Walsh. Officer Noah Walsh," he added.

I slumped back against the tree trunk. "Oh, hey." I smiled weakly. "Could you get that light out of my face, do you think?"

"Sure. Sorry. Are you all right? Are you hurt?" His flashlight shone up and down my body, stopping at the T-shirt wrapped around my ankle.

"Sprain," I explained, struggling to get to my feet.

Officer Walsh stepped forward and wrapped his arm around my waist. "Lean on me."

"Thanks." We began the trek back to the road, easy enough to see now thanks to flashing blue and red lights and multiple flashlights among the trees. "How'd you find me?"

"Your phone pinged off a tower out here. We were patrolling when we found a wet patch of dirt on the road. Saw some scrape marks, assumed there was a struggle. We began searching both sides of the road, but you left an easy trail to follow. Broken branches led me straight to you."

"Oh." I was somewhat deflated that I hadn't hidden as well as I thought I had. "I take it Mills didn't hang around?"

"So, it was Mills who took you? Tell me what happened."

I'd just finished filling him in when we cleared the tree line and stepped out onto the road. Two police cars and an ambulance awaited us. I glanced around for Galloway, all set to lunge into his arms and accept the comfort I deserved, only… no Galloway.

"Audrey Fitzgerald. What have you done to yourself this time?" I glanced up to see my two favorite paramedics headed my way.

"Hey, Ned. Hey, Jayce. Long time, no see."

Ned took Officer Walsh's place, supporting my weight as we hobbled toward the ambulance. "Fellas, I'm fine. My ankle is already strapped, although a little soggy now."

"It's your face I'm concerned about," Jayce said.

My hands flew to my cheeks, feeling for injury. "What's wrong with my face?"

"That's what we need to find out." Jayce climbed into the ambulance first then turned and helped me on board, directing me to the gurney. "Lay down," he ordered.

"I don't need to go to the hospital. I'm fine. Honestly."

Jayce and Ned peered at my face, ignoring me completely. "Some sort of chemical agent?" Ned asked Jayce, who nodded.

Oh! I'd kinda forgotten in all the excitement. "Yeah, I got pepper-sprayed. But I rinsed my eyes out with water. Hence the wet T-shirt. Which got too cold to wear. But since it was cold, I figured I could wrap it around my ankle." I nodded toward the T-shirt currently knotted around my ankle, the bottom of my jeans now damp and cold too. Maybe I didn't really think that one through.

"How do your eyes feel, Audrey?" Jayce asked, flicking a penlight toward my eye and then away again multiple times.

"Fine. Okay, a little sore. Like when you get sand in your eye, and even though the sand is out, your eyeball feels all scratched up still."

Jayce nodded. "Okay, we're going to give you a saline rinse. Rinsing with water straight away was a good move."

"What happened tonight, Audrey?" Jayce asked.

"Urgh. Mills drugged me, tossed me in the trunk of his car, then pepper-sprayed me."

Both men stopped and looked at me. "He drugged you?"

I nodded. "Something in a cloth. Over my mouth and nose."

"Sounds like chloroform," Ned said to Jayce, who nodded in agreement. "Do you have a headache? Nausea? Dizziness?"

"A bit of a headache, but it's been a busy night."

Jayce, the senior of the two paramedics, conferred with his co-worker. "Here's the plan. An eye bath. Oxygen. Examine that ankle. That arm is pretty scratched up, but the abrasions look to be superficial. We'll clean it up and take a closer look. Also, let's get her body temperature up." It wasn't until he mentioned my temperature that I realized I was shaking. A blood pressure cuff was wrapped around my arm, an oxygen mask attached to my face, and then the fun started. Usually, I'm a fan of baths, but eye baths? Not so much. While Jayce thoroughly flushed all toxins from my eyeballs, Ned took care of my ankle.

"Your feet are freezing," he said.

"You know what they say—cold feet, cold heart," I joked. But cold feet came with running around in these temperatures wearing flip flops. After re-strapping my ankle with a fresh, dry bandage, he got a blanket and draped it over me then another one folded double that he wrapped around my feet. I finally relaxed against the gurney, the shivers easing. Ned and Jayce had finished tending to me, the scratches on my hand and arm were cleaned, and like he'd thought, they were superficial and didn't need sutures or dressing. But the oxygen mask remained in place. Personally, I thought it was over-kill. I could breathe fine, but it was nice to lay there for a minute, warm, with freshly washed eyeballs. I bet those babies were sparkling.

The ambulance rocked as the paramedics left and someone climbed on board. I glanced up, hoping to see Galloway. Instead, it was Sergeant Addison Young.

"Oh, wow," she said, eyes glued to my face. I frowned and put a hand up to the oxygen mask. "No," she said, reaching forward to restrain me, "don't touch."

"Why not? What's wrong? Why do you have that freaked out look on your face?" I demanded.

"The paramedics said you'd been pepper-sprayed."

"Yeah? So?"

"Your skin has had a reaction to the spray."

"What? Show me!"

I waited impatiently while the sergeant pulled out her cell phone then handed it to me, the selfie camera activated. I held it up in front of my face and peered at my own image. Nice. Bloodshot eyes were no surprise. But the raw red skin around both eyes was quite the look. Kinda like Bandit,

Thor's new best friend, only instead of a black band around my eyes, mine was red. And kinda gross looking.

Closing my eyes, I handed the phone back to her. "Boys!" I yelled. Jayce and Ned climbed back into the ambulance. "Were either of you going to tell me about my face?" I demanded.

"Your face is fine," Ned said.

"Minor skin irritation from the pepper spray. Why? Is it hurting? I can put some burn gel on it if you want," Jayce said.

I frowned and gently touched the skin around my eyes. It didn't even hurt. Which told me they were right. I wasn't permanently disfigured. "No. It's fine. Doesn't hurt at all."

"Okay, well, we were just telling the detective that you're free to go. I mean, usually, we would take you up to the hospital to be checked over by a doctor, but knowing how you feel about hospitals..."

I grinned. "You got that right. I feel fine. A bit sore, but I'm okay. So, Detective Galloway's here?" I craned my neck, trying to see out the door. Why hadn't he come inside?

"Detective McClain," Sergeant Young explained.

"So, Galloway's *not* here?"

A look of sympathy flashed across the sergeant's face. "Sorry. No."

"But he's back at the station?"

She shook her head. "No, he's on day shift."

Of course, he was. Because I'd seen him at the station myself this morning. So, why, then, wasn't he answering my calls? Surely, word had filtered through to him that I'd been kidnapped by Mills. Despite not being the jealous type, to say I was slightly concerned was an understatement. He couldn't be with Savannah. I absolutely, categorically refused to believe he'd do such a thing.

Chapter Eight

Sergeant Young and Officer Walsh gave me a lift home then announced a patrol car would be stationed out front until they apprehended Mills. I suggested they check the hospital. He possibly had a broken nose and a couple of fractured fingers.

"Where have you been?" Thor demanded, trotting down the hallway, belly swaying from side to side. "And what happened to your face?"

"My face is fine," I told him, limping toward the kitchen. Coffee was in order. And while I knew I should be working on Kira's case, my brain was fried. Truthfully? Mills' attack had rattled me. I couldn't fathom why he'd taken me or what he'd intended to do with me. None of it made any sense, and when things didn't make sense, my brain hurt.

I set about fixing a cup of joe, not caring about the late hour. I wouldn't be able to sleep anyway. Thor jumped on the kitchen counter, a move that would ordinarily get him scolded, but not tonight. Tonight, I could use a little comfort, so I ran my hand over his silky fur, scratched behind his ear, and smiled as his whole body rumbled with a purr.

A sound outside had me whirling around. Was Mills here? Had he arrived before me and had been biding his time, hiding out back until I was alone? I scanned the broad expanse of glass, not seeing anything or anyone. Until a movement caught my eye.

"Bandit." I sagged in relief as the little black and white critter stood on her haunches, front paws up against the glass, staring at us.

"She won't leave," Thor complained, his orange eyes narrowing as Bandit dropped onto all fours and approached the cat door.

"She's lonely. Maybe she doesn't have a family and is all alone."

"Oh." Thor sounded surprised. "I hadn't thought of that."

The cat flap opened, and Bandit's head appeared. "Can I come in?" she asked. I was surprised she'd asked and not just barged in.

"Sure." I beckoned. "But there have to be some ground rules for both of you," I added, giving Thor another pat to assure him I had plenty of love, pats, and kibble for both of them. "Rule one." I held up a finger. "No chasing each other around the house. You wanna play chase, you take it outside. Rule two, stay out of the garbage. Rule three, the inside is not your bathroom. You need to go potty, you take it outside."

"I have never peed inside." Thor sniffed, flicking his tail in irritation.

"May I remind you of the potted palm that used to sit in that corner? The one that mysteriously died?"

Thor ignored me and jumped down from the counter, padding across the floor to Bandit, leaning forward to sniff her nose. "I don't know what you're talking about."

"Will you be my friend?" Bandit said to Thor.

"Hey, you two," I cut in. "Tell me you heard those rules and promise to obey them." I pointed from Thor to Bandit and back again.

"Fine!" Thor grumbled, although why he was grumpy was beyond me. Those had always been the rules—except for chasing each other around the house. Thor had never had a companion before, so this was new to him.

"I will follow the rules," Bandit assured, endearing herself to me even more. Was I crazy, adopting a raccoon as a pet? Absolutely. But I didn't have the heart to shut her outside all alone. And I had a sneaking suspicion Thor liked the interloper more than he cared to admit.

Pulling a cereal bowl from the cupboard, I put a handful of kibble in it and set it next to Thor's bowl. Hopefully, having a bowl each would negate any future squabbles over food. And that cemented it. Bandit was now officially a member of the family. And I must be certifiably insane.

Carrying my coffee to my home office, I eased my weary body into the chair and leaned back, staring at the blank computer screen. Despite the distraction of my attempted abduction, Kira was still missing, and I had work to do, fried brain or not. I wriggled the mouse so the computer woke up, the last program I'd been using displaying on the screen. Kira Melendez's social media. Leaning forward, I pulled up a new page and typed Michael Campbell into the search engine. Pages of results appeared within seconds. Coach had been right. Campbell had been a superstar athlete and was now a very successful businessman. Why, then, had Bill Melendez denied his

daughter the opportunity of working
with him?

I kept digging until my vision blurred,
reminding me my eyeballs had taken a hit
tonight. Jayce had given me some eye drops
if I needed them, and considering I couldn't
read anything on the screen, I needed them.
Hobbling out to the kitchen, I grinned as I
passed Thor and Bandit, curled up together
on the sofa, sound asleep. Seemed the
enemies had changed to friends pretty
quickly.

It took me sixteen tries to get the drops into
my eyes and not onto my face. Eventually, I
succeeded, and I closed my eyes, rolling
them around to distribute the soothing
drops. Blinking them open, I peered around
the living room. Still blurry. I made my way
to the sofa, thinking I'd stretch out with Thor
and Bandit for a few minutes while I waited

for the drops to take effect. Grabbing a couple of spare cushions, I propped one under my ankle, the other under my head, and lay back, closing my eyes for a moment while I went over the case.

I was pretty sure Rowan, the cheating boyfriend, and Eva, the not very good best friend, were not involved. I was also pretty sure I needed to look at Bill and Stephanie Melendez a little more closely. Not that I thought they'd harmed their daughter, but rather... were they the catalyst that caused Kira to run away? It seemed more and more likely, especially if Bill Melendez had rejected Michael Campbell's offer to manage Kira's athletic career.

Interestingly, neither of them had mentioned that when I'd questioned them about Kira's disappearance. Stephanie had been concerned that she'd been distracted with the day spa, spending all her time getting it ready for the grand opening. She hadn't mentioned Michael Campbell at all. And neither had Bill.

I also needed to start thinking about the where. Where had Kira gone? My gut told me I needed to get to the city, specifically a particular high-rise building. Two things held me back. My faulty eyeballs and the relative certainty that if Kira Melendez had turned up on Michael Campbell's doorstep, he'd have at least called her parents.

"Did you know you're a mouth breather and you drool in your sleep?" Ben's voice next to my ear jerked me awake.

"Whaaa?" I slurred, disoriented. I propped myself up on one elbow, careful not to disturb Thor and Bandit, who had relocated from the end of the sofa to snuggle in against my belly. I must have dozed off—sunlight streamed in through the windows. I glanced at the clock on the wall. Seven-thirty.

Flopping back down, I glanced at Ben. "Have you been gone all night?"

He shrugged. "I don't sleep. You don't know it, but I'm gone most nights."

"Where do you go?"

"I check in on Dad. Then I visit the insomniacs who are usually watching Netflix."

I yawned, stretching my arms above my head. Ben's eyes zoomed in on the scratches on my right arm and hand. "What happened to you?"

He didn't mention my face, so I assumed the red mask I'd sported the night before had settled.

"You won't believe it," I said, "but Mills kidnapped me last night." I filled him in on what had happened, then asked, "Is there still a patrol car out front?"

"I'll go check." He was back a solid three seconds later. "Yup."

"Which means they haven't found Mills yet." I sat up, dislodging two furry buddies, who both grumbled in protest and then immediately headed to the food bowls by the back door. They were adorable in their cuteness.

Ben eyed Bandit, one brow raised. "So, this is a thing now?"

"Shut up." My ankle felt marginally better, and I only had a slight limp as I headed for the bathroom. Ben followed, standing outside while I took care of business.

"You haven't asked," he said through the closed door.

"About?"

"Galloway and Savannah."

Oh, that's right. I'd given Ben permission to spy on Galloway and his ex. Not that I thought Kade was up to anything. It was Ben who had trust issues.

"Go on, then," I invited. "Tell me. What did you discover?" I flushed the toilet then washed my hands and examined my reflection in the mirror. The redness had gone, my eyes had their sparkle back, my hair was a mess, and considering the previous twenty-four hours, I actually felt and looked pretty good.

"Well, Kade wasn't with Savannah." Ben's reply was muffled.

I threw open the door and grinned. "See? I told you."

"Yeah, you did." He scuffed a boot silently on the floor.

Which reminded me. I needed a replacement phone thanks to Mills ditching mine in the woods. Galloway had probably been trying to call, only now it was my turn not to pick up. "Where was he, then?" I asked Ben, heading to my office. I'd shoot him an email to explain the phone situation then head into town.

"Dunno," Ben said, following me. "Savannah was watching Die Hard, so I hung out with her."

"I hardly think you can call it hanging out when the other person doesn't even know you're there," I teased, throwing a wink over my shoulder to show I was only kidding. Who was I to begrudge Ben finding entertainment and comfort any way he could? He was a ghost, for crying out loud, his options were limited. I couldn't imagine what it would be like not to be able to talk to people, touch them, eat, drink, sleep. All of my favorite things.

"So, you didn't go to Galloway's place then?"

"Nah. They weren't together. That's all I needed to know."

Flopping onto my office chair, I quickly shot off an email to Galloway explaining the phone situation and reassuring him I was fine. I figured word would have filtered back to him by now about last night. To be honest, I was a little surprised he hadn't turned up on my doorstep. Something important must be going down, to keep him away.

After checking the rest of my emails, I quickly showered, rebandaged my ankle while bolting down my morning caffeine hit, and headed out. First stop, a new phone. Second stop, the Melendezes'.

Chapter Nine

New phone in hand, I stepped inside The Shack, a popular café on Main Street that was usually crowded with patrons. This morning was no exception, with more customers than there were tables. Not that it mattered. I was ordering to go. While waiting my turn in line, I admired my new phone—complete with a glass screen protector and a heavy-duty case that the sales rep assured me would protect the phone in case I dropped it. Which I knew I would at some point. It was a given. In fact, it would be a miracle if I got through today without dropping it.

"Notice how quiet it got when you arrived?" Ben asked conversationally. I glanced up from my phone and looked around to find at least half the patrons staring at me and the other half pretending they weren't.

"What's up with that?" I whispered out the corner of my mouth.

"Dunno."

The line shuffled forward, and a man with a thick body and thin hair stepped away from the counter, takeaway coffee in hand. He stopped when he saw me, giving me the once-over. "Fitzgerald," he said, drawing level.

"Deputy Police Chief," I said in return.

He took a bite out of the donut in his other hand, swallowed, then smirked. "Heard you had an interesting day yesterday."

"You could say that." I wasn't sure what he was getting at, my deposition in the morning or my abduction in the evening.

"You might want to watch yourself."

I cocked my head. Was that a threat? Or friendly advice?

"Thank you, Deputy Police Chief," I said, with an extra degree of pep in my voice. "I'll be sure to do that."

"And for once, Detective Galloway didn't come running to your rescue. I guess he was... otherwise engaged."

I blinked, squared my shoulders, and smiled sweetly. "Thank you for your concern, James, but contrary to what you may believe, not every woman needs a man to save her."

James Clarke was mid-fifties and carried himself with an air of smug superiority. It occurred to me that he may be caught up in the net Galloway and Savannah had cast. It would explain the display of veiled hostility.

He gave me one more leisurely appraisal, took another bite of his donut, then sauntered out the door. The café had been silent throughout our exchange, but as soon as the door swung shut behind him, everyone began speaking at once. Thankfully, not to me. I was back to studying my phone, in particular, looking for missed calls or messages from Galloway. Of which there were none. Now I was starting to get concerned. Twenty-four hours with no contact.

"Morning, Audrey. The usual?"

I glanced up in surprise. It was my turn to order, and I hadn't even noticed the line moving.

I nodded. "Thanks, Andy."

"What was that with Clarke?" Ben leaned an elbow on the counter and surveyed the café.

I lifted the phone to my ear and pretended to be on a call. "What do you mean?"

"That was personal," he pointed out. "That dig about Kade. The insinuation that he's up to something with Savannah."

I shrugged. "You'd know better than I. I haven't had much to do with the man."

"Exactly. He doesn't mean anything to you other than he's the Deputy Police Chief, and when the Police Chief retires, he's got a good shot at getting the top job."

"I have a feeling that wouldn't be a good thing."

Andy slid a takeout cup across the counter. I slid a couple of bills back and waved goodbye, mouthing *thank you* while keeping the phone to my ear. "Something's definitely up."

"Still no word from Kade?" Ben followed me to the door, where a customer quickly jumped up and held it open for me. I smiled my thanks as I passed through.

"No. And I'm starting to get worried. What if something has happened to him?" I glanced around to make sure I couldn't be overheard then dropped my voice anyway. "What if someone found out he's involved in the corruption investigation? What would you do if the heat were on and you were in danger of getting exposed?"

"I'd do anything to shut up the person exposing me."

"Exactly!" My voice went up several octaves, drawing glances from passers-by. I cleared my throat and lowered it back to within normal range. "Mills tried to shut me up. What if he already got to Galloway?"

Ben snorted. "Mills couldn't successfully kidnap you. I find it highly unlikely he managed to get the jump on Galloway."

"Maybe. Look, I need to get to the Melendezes', find their daughter. Could you see if you can find Galloway? Is he holed up at work? I don't care what he's doing. I just need to know that he's safe."

"On it." He turned away then spun back, putting his hand on my shoulder, the coolness of his touch a sensation I wasn't sure I'd ever get used to. "Watch your back today, Fitz. Okay? Mills is still out there, and from all accounts, he has it in for you. While it would be foolish of him to try again, we both know the man is not known for his smarts."

"I will," I promised then fake disconnected the call and slid my phone into the back pocket of my jeans, only to retrieve it minutes later to climb into my car. I tossed it in its usual spot, the cup holder, placed my coffee in the spare holder, and headed to the Ivelisse Day Spa.

The place was looking pretty smart, all ready for the grand opening. The gardeners had finished up, and everything was pristine and sparkling as I walked up the path. I'd half expected to find the place closed, what with Stephanie's daughter missing and all, but the sign on the door said open, so I turned the knob and stepped inside.

I paused for a moment, my eyes adjusting to the low light. Then I spotted him, one elbow leaning on the reception counter, his body angled toward Stephanie, who was in earnest conversation with him. I didn't know who he was, but he looked vaguely familiar. He was also pure male perfection. Not to discredit Galloway, who totally ticked all my boxes, but I'd have to be dead not to appreciate this specimen of manhood in front of me.

Wide shoulders. Lean waist. Chocolate colored hair with caramel highlights. A five o'clock shadow framing a full mouth. Realizing I'd been staring, possibly drooling, I snapped my mouth shut and commanded my legs to get it together and quit mimicking Jell-o.

Stephanie glanced up, saw me, and promptly rushed around the reception desk. "Have you found her?" she demanded.

"I'm sorry. Not yet."

Her whole body deflated as she turned away. The man pulled her into his arms, and she went willingly, collapsing against him, silent sobs wracking her body. Over her head, his impossibly blue eyes locked on me. And that's when it clicked.

"You're Michael Campbell."

He inclined his head, his gaze unwavering. "And you are?"

"Audrey Fitzgerald, Delaney Investigations." I grabbed a card from my purse and handed it to him. "It's fortuitous that you're here."

"Oh?"

"I need to speak with you. You've saved me a trip to the city."

Stephanie pulled out of his embrace and wiped the tears from her face. "Why do you need to speak to Mikey? He doesn't have anything to do with Kira's disappearance."

"You didn't mention that Mr. Campbell offered to take Kira on as a client, to be her manager. And you declined."

Stephanie stiffened. "How do you know about that?"

I tried the arched brow thing again. "I'm an investigator. It's what I do."

"It was Bill who declined," Michael cut in. "As far as I'm concerned, the offer is still on the table. Bill never could get over his small-minded jealousy."

"Jealousy? Over what?" As if it weren't perfectly apparent that Mikey Campbell was an Adonis and every woman's dream. While Bill Melendez was undoubtedly attractive, he didn't quite carry the same magnetism that oozed from Campbell's pores.

"Mikey and I used to date," Stephanie said then barked out a cross between a laugh and a scoff. "In high school! Bill just... he can't accept that I chose him. That I love him. Or that Mikey and I remained friends."

"He seems to think that Steph will eventually come to her senses and realize what a loser he is and come back to me." There was a teasing note in Campbell's voice, and by the way Stephanie punched him in the arm and told him to shut up, I was reasonably sure this had been an ongoing joke for some time.

"You're telling me your husband of . . . what? Sixteen? Seventeen years? Thinks you're going to leave him for your high school sweetheart?" There had to be a reason Bill thought that way. No smoke without fire and all that.

"Fifteen years. We've been married for fifteen years."

Ooooh. Shotgun wedding. I'd bet my last dollar Stephanie was knocked up with Kira when they tied the knot. I didn't miss the look between Stephanie and Campbell. A look that spoke volumes. A look that said the two of them shared secrets. Secrets I was going to have to unearth if I was going to find Kira.

"Could I have a word?" I said to Campbell. "In private."

"Anything you have to say to me can be said in front of her." He postured, shoulders going back, chest thrust out. I almost sighed at what a magnificent chest it was.

"Even if I say that I think Bill is right—that you are indeed still in love with Stephanie?" It was a total guess, but I caught the blush of color across his cheekbones right before the shutters came down.

"What? Don't be ridiculous!" Stephanie cried, storming her way back behind the reception desk, shuffling papers from one side to the other. "Mikey and I are friends. Why can't a man and woman be friends and not have everyone else read something into it?"

"Why indeed?" I agreed with her. Of course I did. Ben and I had been best friends with zero romantic involvement, ever. He was like a brother to me and I a sister to him. But it was different with these two. There was chemistry between them. Although... narrowing my eyes, I studied the blonde-haired woman. Could she be that clueless? Could she not see the love shining so devoutly from this man's eyes? Eyes that were the same sparkling blue as her daughter's?

I may have gasped out loud because both of their heads turned in my direction. I clapped a hand over my mouth, realized how guilty that looked, and quickly lowered it.

"Sorry. Swallowed the wrong way." I coughed, covering the lie, my mind whirling. Coach had said the kids had teased Kira about Bill not being her dad on account of her blue eyes. What if her blue eyes didn't come from her mom? What if they came from Michael Campbell? And what if Michael Campbell dumped his high school girlfriend when she told him she was pregnant because he had a bright future ahead of him, a football career that would see him skyrocket to the stars? A future that did not involve a child.

"You know what?" Campbell said. "I could use a coffee. And I know for a fact that the only caffeine the Ivelisse Day Spa carries is in a body scrub. How about I meet you at the Seaview Café down on the boardwalk, say half an hour?"

I nodded. "It's a date." *Shoot. Not a date. Gah, that sounded like I was flirting with him.* "I mean, not a date, date." *Argh.* Spinning on my heel, I called over my shoulder, "I'll see you there."

Chapter Ten

The Seaview Café was in a lull between the breakfast crowd and the lunch crowd. I'd headed straight there, knowing I'd have time to kill but needing that time to organize my thoughts. And squeeze in an extra coffee. Or two.

I grabbed a table by the window overlooking the bay. The view was breathtaking, and as the days got warmer, we'd see more and more tourists flock to our small town. We were the perfect distance from the city. Close enough to spend the weekend but too far to commute daily.

"Audrey, I'm glad I ran into you."

I glanced up to find Savannah Mcintosh standing by my table, looking tall, stylish, and well-groomed. I tucked a strand of my disheveled hair behind my ear and smiled. "Hey, Savannah, have a seat." I waved at the empty chair across from me, and she slid into it. "What's up? How's the investigation?"

"The investigation is enlightening." She flicked her long shiny hair over one shoulder, and it was as if I were watching a shampoo commercial. Her hair was simply gorgeous. Heck, there wasn't one part of her that wasn't gorgeous. "I heard you had some trouble with Mills," she said, snapping me out of my obsession over her hair.

I'd almost forgotten. If it weren't for the cruiser parked in front of my house, the same one that I suspected was following me around town. There had been a police presence at the Ivelisse Day Spa, and I was sure if I went outside, I'd spot the same cruiser in the parking lot of the boardwalk.

I leaned my elbows on the table. "It's odd that he abducted me."

"Oh? Why do you think that?"

"Because it makes no sense. Kidnapping me would not stop the investigation—plus, I'd already given my deposition. Not that your investigation relies solely on that. I'm just one small piece of a much larger puzzle. So why, then, did Mills snatch me? What was he intending?"

She leaned back and studied me. "Kade was right. You are good."

The waitress appeared with my coffee and asked Savannah if she wanted anything.

"Do you mind? If I join you?" she asked me.

"Of course not. Go ahead."

She ordered a coffee, and after the waitress left, I zeroed in on what Savannah had said earlier about Galloway.

"Have you seen Galloway today?" I asked.

She grinned. "Why do you call him Galloway?"

I shrugged. "Dunno. It was what I called him in the early days, and it just kinda stuck." I narrowed my eyes. Was she avoiding my question?

"Actually, no. I haven't seen him since yesterday," she said.

I slumped back in my chair. Not avoiding my question, then. And Galloway's whereabouts were still a mystery.

"Why do you ask?" she prompted.

I blew out a breath. "Because I haven't heard from him since I left the station yesterday. Which is almost twenty-four hours ago. Don't get the wrong idea, I'm not one of those needy girlfriends, but I am a concerned one. Total silence from him is not normal."

Savannah straightened ever so slightly, the movement almost imperceptible. But I noticed it. Which meant I was right to be concerned. "Has something happened to Galloway?" I demanded.

She held out both palms in a peace gesture. "Not that I know of. But if you're concerned, I can look into it. Find out what he's working on."

I nodded. "Please do. It's not like him not to contact me. Especially after Mills' attack." I glanced out the window at the sun glinting off the ocean. Idyllic. Peaceful. But my brain wouldn't stop with all the what-ifs. What if something terrible had happened and no one knew? No one noticed him missing? I'd assumed he was busy with work, with the internal investigation. But what if he wasn't? What if something nefarious had happened?

Savannah reached across the table and rested her fingers on my wrist, drawing my attention back to her.

"I promise I'll look into it."

I cocked my head and studied her. "What happened with you guys anyway? Why'd you break up?"

She laughed and sat back. "He said you were direct. I like that."

I grinned and waited for her to answer.

"Kade didn't tell you?" she hedged.

"To be honest, the topic of ex-girlfriends never came up. Not until you arrived in Firefly Bay. Stop dodging the question."

"You're astute and tenacious. You should join the force."

"You should stop stalling and answer me. Did he do something bad? Or did you?"

"Neither. It wasn't anything nearly so dramatic. We just realized we liked each other more as friends than lovers." She rolled her shoulders in a dismissive shrug. "We only dated a couple of months. Both of us realized pretty quickly that there was no spark, no fire."

I nodded. Almost like Ben and me, except we hadn't experimented in the lover's department. Eww. But at least Galloway and Savannah had salvaged their friendship from the doomed relationship.

"He's happy with you," Savanna said, drawing me from my thoughts. "The way he lights up when he talks about you? I've never seen that in him before. You're good for him."

"Ditto," I replied, with all the eloquence of a twelve-year-old, then knocked over the salt shaker I'd been fiddling with. Hurriedly righting it, I threw her a grin. "Did he also tell you I'm incredibly clumsy?"

Her lips curled, white teeth flashing in an amused smile. "He may have mentioned it."

"It's a blessing and a curse." I sighed.

"How so?"

For the next twenty minutes, I regaled Savannah with stories of my escapades, the never-ending quest of my sister-in-law, Amanda, to fix me, and my rambunctious family in general. The truth was, I liked Savannah. She was easy to talk to. She had a way of making me feel comfortable, like she was listening—really listening—to what I had to say. No wonder she made a good cop.

"Why did you move to Internal Affairs?" I asked. Once upon a time, she'd been a detective, working alongside Galloway. Why move from working with the cops to investigating them?

"I saw too much." Her mouth turned down at the corners, and it was her turn to play with the salt shaker. "Too much corruption. Payoffs. Criminals doing deals with cops, keeping them out of jail. I couldn't ignore it. But when I reported it to Internal Affairs, I discovered how woefully under-resourced they were. Half of the team didn't want to be there. They'd been transferred because they'd been injured on the job and were deemed unfit for active duty. So, they get shuffled to IA, but they don't wanna be there. They don't want to be investigating their colleagues or stuck behind a desk. Hell, some of them may even be corrupt themselves."

"So, you voluntarily transferred?"

She smirked. "Yep. No regrets."

"And you don't mind that other cops think IA is scum?"

Her smile widened. "I've found that those who really think that are usually the ones who have something to hide."

"Fair point."

"There you are!" Ben approached our table, eyes darting from me to Savannah and lingering. "Where have you been?"

"Right here," I replied, knowing he didn't really expect an answer. His eyes were practically out on stalks as he admired the elegant beauty of Savannah Mcintosh.

"Right here what?" Savannah asked, which was when I realized I'd spoken out loud to Ben without realizing it. *Darn.*

"Sorry. I was talking to myself. I do that sometimes," I explained.

"A lot," Ben cut in.

"A lot," I added.

Savannah leaned back and regarded me with all-seeing eyes. Just how much had Galloway told her about me anyway? He wouldn't have told her about Ben or about me being able to speak to ghosts, surely?

Savannah glanced at her watch. "I need to get back. Thanks for the coffee and chat."

"Yeah, you too." Ben and I watched as she strode away, her long legs covering the floor in sure strides until she'd disappeared from view. Putting my phone to my ear, I jerked my head toward the chair Savannah had just vacated, and Ben slid into it.

"Well?" I asked. "Did you find Galloway?"

I was prepared for him to tell me he had, that Galloway had pulled an all-nighter at the station and all was well. I was not prepared for what he actually said.

"No. I can't. And his place? It looks like there's been a struggle."

"What?"

"Yeah. Coffee table smashed."

"Was there... blood?"

Ben shook his head. "No. Galloway didn't go down without a fight, but I do think something has happened."

"Could this be related to Mills? He botched my abduction, so he took Galloway instead?"

"I find it highly doubtful that Mills could get the jump on Galloway. Especially if you broke his fingers."

"Maybe I didn't break them. Maybe they're just bruised."

"Nevertheless, having your fingers smashed in the trunk of a car is gonna hurt. Doubtful you're going to go get yourself into a fistfight immediately after. Plus, if Mills had any brains, he'd have gone into hiding as soon as he'd realized you'd given him the slip. And finally, Galloway stopped answering your calls before Mills tried to kidnap you."

Good point. I didn't rule him out, but if Mills hadn't taken Galloway, then who? And why?

"I should call Savannah, tell her about this." I lowered my phone, preparing to punch in her number, but Ben reached out to stop me.

"And how, exactly, would you explain it? That you were sitting here with her mere minutes ago, and then you had a premonition that Galloway's apartment has been broken into and he's missing?"

"Well, I wouldn't put it quite like that," I snapped. "She already knows I'm concerned about him, that we haven't had contact for twenty-four hours. She's going to look into it, see what he was working on."

Ben removed his hand from my wrist, which was a blessing because his invisible touch was cold as ice. "Good. That's good."

"Miss Fitzgerald?"

I looked up to see tall, dark, and handsome standing by my table. I blinked, enjoying the view until I suddenly remembered we had a meeting. And here I was, talking to myself.

"Hey." I smiled brightly, no doubt looking like a maniac. "Have a seat. Thanks for meeting with me."

Michael Campbell slid into the seat Savannah had recently vacated. Thankfully, Ben had stood, so Michael wasn't actually sitting on him. I hated it when that happened because I could never manage to hide my reaction. One of utter horror.

"Anything to help Steph get her daughter back."

"You guys went to school together?"

"You've done your homework."

"Of course."

"How can I help?"

"Tell me about your offer to manage Kira Melendez's athletic career. And why Bill Melendez turned it down."

Michael rolled his eyes. "The guy is an insecure idiot."

"Because he's not Kira's father?" I pressed.

Michael threw up both his arms. "Not you too. Man, this rumor has been impossible to kill, spot fires keep cropping up, it's a constant battle to keep putting them out."

I noticed how he didn't deny it. Interesting.

"Let me give you a genetics lesson. Stephanie is a blonde, blue-eyed Caucasian. Bill is an olive-skinned, brown-eyed Mexican. Fifty-fifty shot that Kira is going to have blue eyes," he said.

"Yes, but there's blue eyes, and then there are blue eyes. Stephanie's, while blue, aren't a bright, vibrant blue. Whereas yours? Yours are like sapphires. As are Kira's."

"Ever thought that Kira's eyes look so bright due to her *olive* skin? The contrast?"

Olive skin. I wanted to smack myself on the forehead. If Kira was Stephanie and Michael's offspring, where did her olive complexion come from? Because, while Campbell sported a tan, his overall skin tone was definitely Caucasian.

"Okay, so you're not Kira's dad," I conceded. "Why, then, did Bill turn down your offer to manage Kira?"

"Like I said, he's an insecure idiot."

"But why is he insecure? You and Stephanie dated in high school. That was years ago. Why does that bother him, even now?"

"You're going to have to ask him that." He turned his head away and raised his arm, beckoning the waitress over. "Another?" He nodded his head toward my empty cup.

"Sure, why not?" *Oh, I don't know, because you've already had two in quick succession, and a third might have you strung out and twitching like a rabid squirrel.*

As Campbell conferred with the waitress, I studied him. Yes, he was a good looking and highly successful businessman, but I'd seen the flash of something in his eyes when I'd asked him about Bill. The shutter coming down. And I recognized the distraction technique, calling the waitress over to derail my line of questioning. There was something more to the whole Stephanie, Bill, and Campbell love triangle, and I was determined to get to the bottom of it.

Over coffee, we discussed the proposed contract Campbell offered Kira. It would surely put her on the path to the Olympics. Despite Bill putting the kibosh on the whole thing, Campbell had left the offer open indefinitely.

"I'm sure Kira wants her dad to agree." I picked up my cup and took a sip, noticing the slight tremor. Caffeine was kicking in now. I hurriedly put the cup back down before I spilled the contents. "Why can't Stephanie sign it instead?"

"Kira is a minor. Both parents need to sign the contract. For this to work, they have to be united in their goal."

"But Bill *does* want to see his daughter reach the Olympics, to win gold for her country."

"Of course he does," Campbell agreed. "Just not with me."

And again, we were back to the personal relationship between the three adults.

"Have you heard from Kira recently? She hasn't called or emailed or suggested she wants to meet with you?"

He shook his head. "Nope."

I leaned back in my chair, palms cupping my coffee cup. Things weren't adding up, and I hated it when that happened. Kira had run away, yet I couldn't fathom why. Yes, her boyfriend had cheated on her with her best friend, but Kira had already dumped him. And it was doubtful she knew about the cheating. And even if she did, why run away? Kira didn't strike me as an over-emotional hormone-driven teenager.

"You're good friends with Stephanie?" I broke the silence that had settled between us.

"Mmmhmm."

"How are things at home? Does she talk to you about Bill?" It was a long shot. Would a woman confide in an ex-boyfriend about her current marital issues? Possibly.

He lifted one shoulder. "The guy can be a moron, but she loves him, and as long as Steph's happy, that's all I care about. But if he hurts her, if he breaks her heart..." he trailed off, the unspoken threat hanging in the air.

"You'll what? Swoop in and play the hero? Are you still in love with her?"

He drained his coffee in one gulp and placed the cup down on the table with precise movements. "We're done here."

"You are, aren't you?" He so was. It was all over his face, the angry twist of his mouth, the flush of color on his cheekbones, the way his hands clenched into fists. He was on his feet, digging in his wallet. He threw some bills on the table and stalked away without another word.

Chapter Eleven

I watched him leave, feeling kinda sad for him. I wondered if Stephanie knew he still cared so deeply for her. Bill wasn't a moron. He was a smart man who knew Campbell was waiting in the wings, ready to swoop in and steal his girl should he ever make a misstep. But what did all of that have to do with Kira's disappearance?

I stood and immediately clenched my knees as gravity got the better of my bladder.

Three coffees in quick succession would do that to a girl. Hurrying toward the bathroom and ignoring the twinge in my ankle that was reminding me with each step that I wasn't healed yet, I almost landed on my rear when I ran into someone, ricocheting off them with an *oomph*.

"Oops! So sorry, I wasn't looking where I was going." Ashley Baker grabbed my arm to steady me, her long blonde dreadlocks swinging forward. Ashley owned the new age store along the boardwalk, Nine, and had given me an incredible massage once when I'd been injured after rolling my car. Ben's car. I'd totaled it and managed to bruise myself pretty spectacularly in the process. But Ashley and her healing oils and hands had worked miracles.

"No problem." I smiled while maneuvering around her. The bathroom situation was somewhat urgent at this point, my pelvic floor muscles screaming in protest.

"Audrey, wait." Ashley kept a hold of my arm. "What's up with you? Your aura is all wrong."

I leaned forward and hissed, "I really need to pee."

"Oh. Right, sorry." She released my arm, and I hurried away, calling over my shoulder, "Good to see you, Ashley. I may drop into Nine and pick up some more of those massage oils."

"Yeah, sure." She waved and continued to the cash register while I half bolted, half duck waddled with my knees clamped together, bursting into the bathroom and an empty stall. Thank goodness there wasn't a line!

Ben joined me. Not in the stall but outside of it. I could see his feet under the door.

"So, not only do we have a missing teenager, we have a missing boyfriend, too," he said.

"What? Who?" *Don't tell me Rowan has disappeared as well.*

"I was talking about Galloway, you idiot."

"Oh." I cleared my throat. "Right." I knew that. "Well... Kira is my priority. Galloway can take care of himself." Not that I wasn't worried. I was. But Galloway was a cop. He had training, and he had a bunch of colleagues who'd be searching for him if they weren't already. I'd alerted Savannah that something was up, and when he didn't turn up for work, someone would go looking. They'd find what Ben had. Signs of a struggle. And the search would begin. I had to trust that they would find him safe and sound. I couldn't let myself contemplate anything else. *He's fine* was a mantra playing over and over in my head.

But Kira? I wasn't sure foul play was involved in her disappearance, but I couldn't rule it out. Wherever she'd gone, she'd gone voluntarily. But her behavior was out of the norm. To not tell her parents where she was going, not come home, ditch school and training? All of that, according to everyone I'd spoken to, was out of character.

"To tell you the truth," I said to Ben, "I'm stumped. The only good news is that she's not dead."

"How do you know that?"

"No ghost. Every case I've had that involves a dead body comes with the victim's ghost. But so far, I have not seen ghostly Kira, which tells me she's alive." For now.

Ben began pacing. "That's good. Not dead. But what if she's being held against her will?"

"It doesn't look like anyone took her," I pointed out, finishing up and flushing the toilet. "She wasn't kidnapped. She ran away."

"A kidnapper could have made it look that way."

"You think someone broke into her home, emptied out her school bag, and shoved clothes in it to make it look like she'd run away? And then they, what, snatched her? Yet no contact with Steph or Bill. No ransom demand."

Flinging open the door to the stall, I came face-to-face with Lacey Stevens.

"Oh!" I blinked in surprise. "Hey, Lacey." I shot Ben a look. He could have warned me someone had come in. He waved his hand in a *yeah whatever* gesture, and if he weren't already dead, I could have happily killed him.

"Audrey. Talking to yourself again?" Lacey arched a brow and brushed past. Lacey was in her late forties and a cougar. I'd had dealings with her in a previous case when her best friend had died, and I'd discovered Lacey had been dating her son.

"Lacey. Scoping out the competition?" I shot back. Lacey was also a chef at the Firefly Bay Hotel.

"Of course. Gotta stay current, and the best way to do that is to visit other restaurants and cafes as a patron. It's not just the food; it's the service and ambiance that, combined, make the dining experience a good one. Or not." She closed the door of the stall, and I heard the lock slide into place.

I quickly washed and dried my hands and headed out, phone to my ear.

"You could have warned me," I said to Ben as he strolled by my side, hands in pockets.

"Where would the fun be in that?" he teased. I elbowed him in the side, which achieved precisely nothing other than to make me lose my balance and stagger as I shied away from the icy sensation. He laughed. I looked like an idiot.

Outside on the boardwalk, I paused for a moment, enjoying the warmth of the sun and the smell of the ocean. "It's a beautiful day." I sighed.

"Sure is." Ben leaned on the railing and looked into the water below.

I joined him, watching the waves ebb and flow as they washed against the pylons supporting the boardwalk. It'd be summer soon enough, lazy days enjoying ice cream. It was something Ben and I had indulged in frequently, and it saddened me to know we wouldn't be having ice cream together ever again.

A cold blast against my rib cage told me he'd just nudged me. I turned my head to look at him.

"You're doing it again," he said.

"What?"

"Getting maudlin. Don't be sad. I'm still here."

"But you're not *here* here."

"A little bit here is better than no here at all."

"True."

"It'll get easier," he promised.

"Will it, though?"

He smiled. "Yeah. Of course. Because this," he waved his hand around, "is a first. Everything so far has been a first. Your first winter without me. First Christmas without me. First spring without me. Next year, it'll be easier."

I hoped so because I missed my best friend terribly. My heart constantly ached at the loss. But he was right. Having ghost Ben was better than no Ben at all.

"Oh, hey again, Audrey. You waiting for me?" Ashley Baker approached with a light jingle accentuating every step. I glanced down. Beneath her long flowing skirt was an ankle bracelet sporting a dozen tiny bells.

"Umm." I wasn't. "Sure." May as well grab some more of that massage oil she'd whipped up for me last time. It may just help my ankle heal a little faster.

"Come on in."

I followed her to the door of Nine, which was locked, with a back in five minutes sign taped to the glass. She unlocked it and ushered me inside. Nothing had changed aside from the odd display that now housed different products.

"How have you been, Ashley?" I asked, perusing the shelves while she watched me, taking a sip every now and then from her takeout cup. I liked Ashley. I liked that she didn't conform. She wore what she wanted— today, it was a green ankle-length skirt, a tie-dye tank in a riot of blues, greens, and yellows, and a fuchsia pink cardigan that she'd stretched and tied in a knot at her waist. Beneath one sleeve of the cardigan, I caught a glimpse of her tattoos.

She tossed her waist-length dreadlocks over her shoulder. She wore them loose today.

Some days, they were piled high on top of her head with a scarf wrapped around to hold them in place. "All good here. Are you on another case?" She stopped and sucked in a breath. "Has someone died?"

"Yes, I'm on a case, but no, no-one's died," I reassured her. "Missing person."

"Oh, anyone I know?"

I glanced around the new age shop with its candles, crystals, and incense. I highly doubted Kira had any use for items like this, but it was worth a shot. "Kira Melendez. Know her?"

"Melendez? That name rings a bell." She tapped her lip, eyes raised to the ceiling, and I could practically see her mind flipping through a mental Rolodex, searching.

"Stephanie and Bill's daughter," I added.

She snapped her fingers. "Yes, of course. Stephanie has just opened that new day spa, Ivelisse, right?"

"That's right."

"She's done a good job. The renovation is lovely, and I hear business is good."

"You hear?" I paused in studying a crystal, carefully putting it back on the shelf.

"Sure. We're not in direct competition, but we're both in the health and wellness industry."

Right. I hadn't considered that. The Ivelisse day spa had sported candles and incense and relaxing music, much like what I could hear coming from the speaker mounted at the rear of Nine.

"I know Holly was a little put-out, having another spa open up," Ashley continued.

"You want the massage oil for muscle strains, yes?"

"Yeah, please. And who's Holly?"

"Holly Wilson. She runs the Divine Delights Spa & Resort. I don't know why she was so stressed over Stephanie's spa. Holly offers an entirely different experience. You go there for an overnight stay or a whole weekend and immerse yourself in it. Massages, yoga, facials. She makes a roaring trade with bridal parties. Stephanie's place doesn't offer anything like that. She's your standard operating hours type of spa."

I remembered where I'd heard Holly's name before. It was printed on a crumpled flyer in Kira's drawer. Stephanie had said she'd visited all the local and not so local spas to scope out the competition. We'd written off the flyer being in Kira's drawer as accidental. Scooped up with a bunch of take-out menus, but now I wondered if there weren't more to it.

"Here you go." Ashley placed a small brown bottle on the counter. "Can I help you with anything else?" She peered at me, eyes assessing from top to toe. "An aura cleaning, perhaps?"

I grimaced. "I'm fine, thanks." After paying for my purchase, I joined Ben outside. He was leaning one elbow on the balustrade and eyeballing the boutique shop next door to Nine. It was vacant, with a For Lease sign in the window. Previously, it had been a psychic's store, Nether & Void; only the owner—and apparent psychic—had been murdered. The place had been vacant ever since.

"This is prime real estate," I said. "I would have thought someone would have snatched this up by now."

Ben sighed. "No one wants to lease a shop where a woman was murdered. Bad ju-ju."

"Well, we know it's not haunted. Myra crossed over." Myra Hanson was the psychic who hadn't seen her own death coming. Her ghost had hung around while we investigated her murder, but as soon as I'd outed the guilty party, Myra had moved on.

"Got your oil?" Ben asked, falling into step beside me as I made my way along the boardwalk, heading toward the parking lot.

"Yep. This stuff really helps with sore muscles and bruising. I'm going to try and remember to always keep some on hand."

"You should order a crate of the stuff."

"Har har." Everyone's a comedian.

I'd just stepped from the wooden boardwalk onto the asphalt of the parking lot when my personal protection police cruiser that was currently parked two spaces behind my car flipped on its red and blue flashing lights, activated its siren, and tore out of the parking lot at speed.

"Wonder what that's about?"

It was a rhetorical question, but Ben answered anyway. "Dunno."

Thank you, Ben. So enlightening.

I didn't give the cop car much thought as I drove home. Instead, my mind was full of Kira Melendez, her parents, Michael Campbell, and now, Holly Wilson.

"I'm probably grasping at straws," I said, tapping the steering wheel as I traversed the streets on autopilot.

"What straws?" Ben asked.

"The whole Holly Wilson thing." I sighed. Was there a connection?

"Who's Holly Wilson? What thing?"

"Oh, right. You weren't there. So, I found a flyer for a day spa run by Holly Wilson. It was in Kira's drawer. Stephanie thinks it got caught up with a pile of take-out menus, that Kira hadn't put it in her drawer intentionally."

"Right." His tone said he was waiting on the rest because what I'd told him so far was not enlightening in the least.

"But I was just chatting with Ashley, and she mentioned Holly's name and that apparently Holly was put-out about a new spa opening up."

"Gotcha. You're wondering if there's a link?"

I shrugged. "It's pretty tenuous. Possibly nothing, but I'm adding it to the file. Stephanie visited Holly's spa as part of her research. Maybe something happened. Maybe there's bad blood between them."

"And what? Holly kidnapped Kira as payback?" Ben scoffed, clearly thinking the whole idea was ludicrous. He was right. So what if there was bad blood? I'd hardly think Holly would kidnap her rival's daughter. Dueling facials perhaps but not kidnapping.

Chapter Twelve

The Cheez-its scattered on the hallway floor were the first sign that something was amiss. Picking my way over the cheesy snacks, I made my way to the rear of the house where the open plan living, dining, and kitchen were located. And where Armageddon part two had taken place.

"Bandit! Thor!" I yelled, tossing my bag onto the dresser and standing with my hands on my hips.

"Oh, boy," Ben said. "Bandit got into the pantry."

Seems I'd learned something new—raccoons can open doors. Because I knew for a fact the pantry door had been shut. I keep it closed to keep Thor out. Shaking my head, I made my way through the torn open packets of pasta and flour, half-eaten packet of cookies, and decimated coconut. Standing in the open doorway of the pantry, I flicked on the light.

Thor blinked sleepy eyes at me from the third shelf where he was curled up against the potatoes. I scanned for Bandit but couldn't see her.

"Where's Bandit?" I demanded.

"She's here somewhere." Thor yawned.

"I'm here!" Bandit popped out from behind the blender on the bottom shelf.

I eyeballed the furry critters, who were clearly shaking off the effects of a food coma. "New rule. No pantry. Ever."

"What's a pantry?" Bandit asked while Thor closed his eyes and went back to sleep.

"This," I waved my arm around, "is a pantry. It's where I keep the food. Human food. And while we're at it, the refrigerator is off-limits too."

"What's a refrigerator?"

"It's the big metal box over there. It's where the chicken is. And eggs," Thor mumbled.

"Is there mango?" Bandit asked. "I couldn't find any here." She bustled out of her hiding spot behind the blender, her belly round. I really hoped it was due to food and not babies.

Heaving a sigh, I grabbed the broom and shooed the pair of them outside while I got to cleaning up the unholy mess they'd made. But there was something about cleaning floors and taking out the trash that was cathartic. It gave me time to think. While I was cleaning, I pondered the Melendez family, and something occurred to me. I hadn't done a deep dive into their background, merely skimmed the surface. For starters, how had Stephanie financed the Ivelisse Day Spa? Bill had a landscaping business, but it was a relatively small concern. I'd find it highly doubtful he had enough equity in his business to finance hers. Had they mortgaged the house?

By the time I was done cleaning, my ankle was throbbing, my caffeine buzz had worn off, and I'd started a shopping list to replace all the items the two terrors had torn into. I suspected Bandit was the one doing all the tearing; Thor knew better, but he'd gone along for the ride, and the reward when they found treats they liked.

Easing myself into my office chair, I propped my ankle up on the corner of the desk then began digging into the Melendezes' finances. I didn't have to search far. It seemed Stephanie Melendez had a partner in the spa. Interesting that she hadn't mentioned it.

I picked up the phone and called her. "Why didn't you tell me you had a partner in Ivelisse?" I asked without preamble.

"Silent partner," she said. "And how did you find out, anyway? No one is supposed to know."

"Including your husband?"

She remained silent for so long I thought we'd been disconnected. "Hello?"

"Especially my husband," she eventually said.

"Are you and Campbell having an affair?"

"What? No! Absolutely not." Her protest seemed genuine. And she hadn't dodged the question. A promising sign she was telling the truth.

"Then why has he financed Ivelisse Day Spa?" That was a beyond generous gesture on Campbell's behalf. Was there something in it for him other than a business deal?

"Because he's a good friend. Okay, look, I know it looks bad that Bill doesn't know." Agitation was evident in her voice. "But Bill just has this jealousy over Mikey, and he hates that we've remained friends. We decided it would be best if Mikey were a silent partner and that we'd keep it between the two of us. No one else needs to know."

"Pretty big secret to keep. Especially when it's relatively easy to find out the truth should you care to go looking" I pointed out. "Risky even."

"I didn't have a choice. When I lost my job, I thought it'd be easy to get another. I'm a qualified beauty therapist, but the salons and spas only wanted pretty young things. No one wanted me."

I scoffed. "I'd hardly call you old. Or unattractive." Stephanie was in her forties and gorgeous.

"Yes, but someone with my level of experience means a higher pay grade."

"Wait. So, all the spas you were visiting weren't really for research. You were looking for work?"

She sighed. "Yes. And then Mikey called, telling me Bill had contacted him and told him to shove Kira's contract where the sun doesn't shine, and it was all too much, the stress of it. I told him I was out of work, couldn't find a job, and while Bill's business does okay, we can't survive on the income it brings in. Not if we want to keep our house and send Kira to college and pay for the training she needs."

"And that's when he cooked up a plan to finance Ivelisse."

"I'll pay him back. But it'll take time. In the meantime, I run Ivelisse as my own. Mikey had his financial planner meet with me so we could create a solid business plan. Mikey doesn't want to know the details and doesn't want to be involved. He's just fronting the money and any business expertise his own company can provide. I'm not his only investment. He owns or partially owns several small businesses and two hotels. He has a solid team behind him."

"You don't need to convince me." I removed the Ace bandage from my ankle to see how the swelling and bruising was going. Answer? Spectacular. Still swollen and now a lovely shade of purple and black. No wonder it hurt. "That sounds like a spiel you have ready for your husband."

"Possibly."

"Definitely." But did it involve Kira and her disappearance? Not really. None of them had a motive for hiding the teenager. If Bill and Stephanie had split, I'd automatically suspect one of them of keeping their daughter from their ex-spouse. However, Stephanie was adamant her marriage was stable, despite her high school ex being in her life and still madly in love with her. As for Michael Campbell, forcing Stephanie's hand by taking her daughter was not a smart move, and one thing I'd learned was that

Campbell was a very smart cookie. It wasn't him.

Which brought me back around to the only other clue. Holly Wilson. All I had was a flyer found in Kira's room and gossip that Holly had not been happy about Stephanie opening a spa in competition with her. Was that reason enough to... what? Kidnap Kira? I was grasping at straws that this was a kidnapping. All the evidence pointed to Kira running away, yet my sixth sense told me that wasn't the case. This was a girl who was utterly devoted to her athletic training. She wouldn't just abandon it. In fact, Kira struck me as the type of girl who had a plan. She'd wear her father down until she got him to agree to Michael Campbell being her manager. Was part of that plan to disappear for a few days?

"Are you there?" Stephanie's voice in my ear reminded me the call was still connected.

"Yeah, sorry, I was thinking. How well do you know Holly Wilson?"

"Holly?" she said in surprise. "Not that well. I know of her, of course. I visited her spa. She didn't have any vacancies, and to be honest, the hours at Divine Delights wouldn't have worked for me anyway. I don't want to be working evenings and weekends."

"Did she know you were thinking of opening your own spa?"

"No. Because at that time, I wasn't. It wasn't until later, when I couldn't find a job, that Mikey came up with the idea."

Interesting. So, the idea of Ivelisse hadn't been Stephanie's. It had been Campbell's. I wrapped up the call and leaned back in the chair, staring at the ceiling, lost in thought.

"Ben?" I didn't even know if he was still in the house. I'd seen him in my peripheral vision while I'd been cleaning, but since he couldn't help me, I hadn't paid him any attention.

"Yeah?" He appeared in the doorway.

"Just to cover all my bases, can you check out Campbell's office and home and check that he doesn't have Kira squirreled away?"

"I can try. I've never traveled that far before. Not sure if it's possible."

"Right. Good point." So far, Ben had only transported around Firefly Bay. The city was an hour's drive. Was it too far for Ben's paranormal abilities? If it was, I'd jump in my car and drive there myself.

"You're thinking Campbell's good for this?" he asked, one eyebrow raised.

"Actually, no, I don't."

"But better safe than sorry?"

"Exactly."

"I'm on it." He disappeared before my eyes, leaving me with my thoughts. With only one last thread to tug on, I decided a visit to Divine Delights Spa & Resort was in order.

After rebandaging my ankle, I popped a couple of painkillers, punched the address for the Divine Delights Spa & Resort into Google Maps, and headed out. One thing Holly offered with her treatments was tranquility, and seeing that her spa was out in the middle of nowhere, I was pretty sure she achieved the serene status she was going for. According to the app on my phone, it would take me thirty-six minutes to reach my destination, so I set up some tunes and let my mind drift as I drove.

It didn't drift far. Mostly thoughts of Galloway and trying not to worry. Still, anxiety gnawed at my stomach, and if I went too far down the *what-if* road, I was certain I'd puke. *He's fine*, I chanted to myself. Interspersed with thoughts of Galloway were some of Kira. If the Holly lead was a dead end, then my only recourse was to visit anyone who lived in the vicinity of the Melendezes and ask if they had CCTV. It would be long and laborious, but someone must have seen something. A camera may have caught her walking past or hitching a ride. A girl simply didn't disappear off the face of the earth.

The sudden jerking of my vehicle snapped me to attention. Clenching the steering wheel with both hands, I fought for control as the back end slid around, almost off the road, before I managed to swing it back. Of course, I over-corrected and was in danger of sliding off the other side as I fishtailed at great speed on the open highway. A quick glance in my rearview told me the cause of my problems. A big, black truck was tailgating me. He must have clipped my bumper, nearly sending me tail spinning off the road.

He backed off, and I rolled my shoulders and flexed my fingers, shaking off the tension in my muscles. That had been close. Whoever it was behind me must have been distracted not to see me on the road in front of him. Only that didn't seem to be the case because I glanced up to see the truck approaching again, at speed. I braced myself. He was going to ram me.

The crunch of metal on metal and the screeching of tires were all I could hear. This hit was harder. More aggressive. And he didn't back off. I'd slammed my foot on the brake out of pure reflex, yet he was pushing me along the road. Or more precisely, pushing me off. My car was starting to turn on an angle, and if he kept this up, I'd roll.

Think, think, think. But it was hard to think clearly with someone hell-bent on pushing you off the road. My heart was thundering in my chest, and I was bathed in sweat. I eased my foot off the brake and back onto the accelerator. If I could accelerate away from him, he wouldn't be able to push me anywhere.

It worked! Flying down the highway, our vehicles disconnected, and I inched forward, slowly increasing the gap between us. Of course, that meant my speed was increasing, and there was a corner up ahead. I took it on two wheels, gritting my teeth until my SUV bounced back onto all four wheels. While the black truck was still behind, he was losing ground. Whatever game he was playing, he was losing. Thank goodness.

So, of course, when my rear windshield exploded into a million pieces of glass, I screamed and almost peed myself. I lost control of the car, zig-zagging across the road, frantically spinning the wheel to regain control, and failing. I flew down into a ditch, the hood burying itself in the dirt while I catapulted forward. The last thing I remember is my head striking the steering wheel.

Chapter Thirteen

I woke up with a thundering headache and unable to move my limbs. Great. I'd finally done it. Injured myself so severely I was now a vegetable. Amanda would have a field day with this one.

"Audrey?" someone whispered. I frowned. It sounded like Galloway. I cracked open one eye, expecting to find myself in a hospital bed. Instead, I was in a dimly lit... what? Warehouse? Where the heck was I? I lifted my head and groaned at the pain in my neck.

"Audrey, you okay?" It *was* Galloway!

I turned my head, my neck muscles protesting the movement. "Whiplash," I whispered to him. He was tied to a chair, his face and clothes bloody.

"Fixable," he whispered back, his gray eyes dark with concern.

"Are you okay?"

"I'm fine. I'm more worried about you. That's a nasty wound on your forehead."

I went to touch my hand to my forehead, but again found I couldn't move. Looking down, I discovered why. I, too, was strapped to a wooden chair, each wrist bound to the arms, my ankles strapped to the legs. I looked around again. It was dim, and the place stank of rotten fish.

"Are we at the docks?" I kept my voice low. I thought we were alone, but anyone could be lurking in the shadows, listening to our exchange. As I moved my head, I felt something warm and wet trickle over my eyebrow and drop onto my cheek. "Am I bleeding?" My voice went up an octave, and I bit my lip to silence myself.

"Yeah," Galloway whispered. "Did Redding hit you?"

"With his car. Wait. Redding? As in?"

"Detective Sergeant Joel Redding," Galloway confirmed. So, it hadn't been Mills behind me on the highway, hip and shouldering my car off the road.

"So, he's..."

Galloway nodded. "Yep. One of the bad guys."

"And we're here because?"

A door to the left flung open, smashing against the wall. "Because the two of you don't know how to keep your noses out of other people's business," a voice boomed. The stream of light silhouetted a big man with a soft body. I narrowed my eyes, trying to get a good look at his face, but with the light to his back, it was impossible to see his features.

"I don't know what you think you're going to accomplish with this, Clarke," Galloway snapped, "but it's going to backfire spectacularly."

Clarke? Did he say Clarke? My head swiveled from Galloway to the shadowed man and back again. Not a good thing when you're suffering whiplash. But Galloway had said Clarke... as in Deputy Police Chief James Clarke? The very same man I'd bumped into this morning. Had he had Galloway all along? Was he behind the smear campaign that Galloway was cheating on me with Savannah? The pounding in my head increased.

"Hard to be charged with murder if they never find the bodies," Clarke drawled.

My head whipped around to stare at Galloway, aghast. "Murder?" I mouthed, eyes wide.

He gave a slight shake of his head as if assuring me it would all be okay and that we would not end up dead. While I really wanted to believe him, considering both of us were currently tied to chairs, Clarke most definitely had the upper hand. I turned my attention back to the obnoxious man as he sauntered inside. On his heels was Detective Sergeant Joel Redding.

Now, Redding had been a surprise. Was this it? Was this little gang of toxic egos and abuse of power the corruptness that was poisoning Firefly Bay PD? No, we were missing Mills. And Sergeant Dwight Clements. He had to be involved somehow. He'd been riding my butt as hard as Mills, determined to bring me down.

"I'd like to see how you think you're going to dispose of two bodies without being discovered." Galloway sneered.

Clarke laughed, an ugly sound, and pulled a pistol from where it had been tucked into the back of his waistband. I swallowed, nausea burning the back of my throat. My pulse was hammering so hard I expected my head wound to literally start squirting blood out in copious quantities, but strangely, it didn't. It just continued to trickle slowly down my face and drip onto my shirt.

As Clarke approached, the door slammed open again, hitting the wall with a loud bang.

Wherever we were, it was away from civilization. These men were making no effort to keep the noise down. Mills tore into the warehouse with a bone to pick. Or a bone to break. Either way, he was testy. He headed straight for me, elbowing past Clarke, who looked at him with surprise.

"The gang's all here," I sneered.

Mills backhanded me across the face so hard my teeth rattled.

"Hey!" Galloway shouted. "How 'bout you pick on someone your own size?"

Mills ignored him, drawing his arm back to deliver another blow when Clarke yelled, "Enough!"

Mills froze, and something flashed in his eyes. Pain, perhaps. Homicidal tendencies? It was hard to tell.

"We're killing them anyway," he spat. "I say we do it now. And I want her. I want to make her suffer. I want to make her feel pain like she's never felt before. I want her to beg."

Had I heard him correctly? My ears were still ringing from the blow he'd delivered, but I was pretty sure he'd just said he wanted me to beg for my life.

"I thought you would have learned by now that we can't always have what we want," I drawled then braced myself for another blow. Why I was antagonizing him? I didn't know, but I couldn't seem to stop myself. Clarke stepped closer to Mills, and Mills stepped closer to Clarke, until they were up in each other's business.

I shot Galloway a look. He was trying to tell me something. His eyes were darting around, and he was mouthing something. Eggs for dinner? But that didn't make sense.

My heart jolted when he threw himself backward, both he and the chair landing on the floor with a crash. The chair splintered, and Galloway leaped to his feet, ropes dangling, the arm of the chair clasped in his hand. Once a constraint, now a weapon.

Chaos erupted. Clarke and Mills turned toward Galloway, but before Clarke could even raise his arm to aim the gun, Galloway had slammed the piece of wood into the side of Clarke's head. He staggered back, blood streaming. In a whir of motion, he attacked Mills, and then things blurred as the three of them went down in a scuffle, with Redding standing back, watching the fray with arms crossed.

Three against one was not fair odds. Deciding to follow Galloway's lead, I pushed on the floor with my toes until my chair toppled backward. I hit the floor, my head bounced off the concrete, and I saw stars, but I heard the chair break and quickly wriggled free. Or tried to. One of the chair's arms had broken. The other was still intact with my wrist tied to it and both ankles to the legs, so I was now lying on my back with my legs in the air like a turtle. With a bit of wriggling and finagling, I eventually got loose.

Mills was out cold on the floor. Clarke and Galloway were locked together in mortal combat, yet Redding still stood back, making no move to hinder or assist. The gun was on the floor, so I scuttled over, picked it up, and fired a shot into the ceiling.

The sound was so loud I feared I'd permanently damaged my hearing, but it did the trick. Both men froze, turning to face me. Galloway quickly crossed to my side and cupped his big hand over mine, sliding the gun from my trembling fingers.

"Glad you aimed at the ceiling," Galloway whispered in my ear.

"I didn't. I aimed at Clarke."

"You what?" His eyes were huge, but then I winked, and he barked out a laugh.

I don't know why I was cracking jokes at a time like this. Possibly one too many blows to the head, I decided. I was probably concussed. Or brain damaged. Maybe none of this was real. Maybe I was in a hospital bed, in a coma, and all of this was a product of my imagination.

I felt it before I heard it. The whiz of a bullet, the searing hot pain in my upper arm, followed by a bang. We'd forgotten about Redding.

"Shit," Galloway hissed, grabbing my other arm and dragging me across the floor. A hail of bullets followed our progress, but Redding must have had his eyes shut, for not a single shot made its mark. Well, if you didn't count that first one. Thankfully, it didn't hurt, but when I glanced down, I saw the hole in the sleeve of my T-shirt. And the blood. Rather a lot of blood.

We burst through the door on the opposite side of the warehouse, and Galloway slammed it closed behind us. Bullets continued to ping through the flimsy walls.

Galloway started to take off but turned and grabbed my shoulder and pulled me close. With his mouth barely inches from mine, he said, "Keep your head down and try to keep up."

"Gotcha." Keep my head up and try to keep down. I could do that. He took off at a run, and I followed. Not at a run. My ankle refused to carry my weight, pain burning through me with each failed attempt. I must have damaged it further in the car crash because the sprain had been healing nicely. No reason I couldn't hobble at a semi-decent pace behind Galloway.

I could just make him out. He looked small in the distance. He hadn't realized I wasn't behind him. Instead, I was on my hands and knees attempting to follow, only my arm was starting to sting like the blazes, my vision was blurry, and I had the horrifying realization that I may just be screwed.

"Jeez, Audrey! Why didn't you tell me it was this bad?" Galloway was back, crouched in front of me.

Grabbing his shirt, I hauled myself to my feet. "I'm okay," I said. The world was only spinning a little. How bad could it be?

"Change of plan." Galloway tucked the gun in his belt then scooped me over his shoulder in a fireman's hold. I would have relished the close contact with him if it weren't for the fact that I was upside down with his shoulder digging into my belly, concentrating very hard on not tossing my cookies. We hadn't gone far when he lowered me to the ground, propping my back against a tree.

"Stay here," he whispered, running a hand over my cheek and tucking some hair behind my ear. "Don't make a sound. I'll be back."

As much as I wanted to disobey instructions and join in the fray, my body shut that idea down. I was reasonably confident my limbs would not obey any requests for movement, so I sat, and I listened as gunshots were exchanged and pushed down my fear that Galloway could be shot. Worse, killed. The adrenaline coursing through my veins kept the pain at bay, but I knew it was waiting at the edges, waiting to consume me. My ankle was wrecked, I had a head wound, and I'd been shot. I was delighted I could not feel all three. As it was, I sat with my free hand clamped over the gunshot wound, but blood still flowed from beneath my fingers. I really hoped I didn't bleed to death out here.

I was starting to doze off when Galloway returned.

"Hang on," he said then scooped me off the ground and into his arms. This time not in a fireman's hold. This time, I was clasped to his chest, and it was lovely.

I turned my face into his warmth and breathed him in. "I missed you," I murmured.

"I missed you too." I felt his kiss on the top of my head, then we were back at the warehouse, which turned out not to be a warehouse at all but an old barn. I'd sworn I'd smelled fish. I'd thought we were at the docks, but I'd been way off. Police lights flashed, there were a barrage of voices that I couldn't make out, lots of jostling and poking and prodding, and then the wave of pain descended like a tsunami. My blood pressure spiked then dropped, and my eyes rolled into the back of my head as oblivion claimed me.

Chapter Fourteen

I woke up in a hospital bed, a drip in my arm, a cast on my leg, and an odd numb type sensation throughout my entire body.

"Galloway?" I croaked through dry lips. My mouth tasted like I'd licked an ashtray.

"He's fine. In better shape than you." Savannah Mcintosh sat in a chair by the side of my bed, flicking through a magazine.

I turned my head. "Where is he?"

"Just finishing up some business. He'll be here soon. He wanted to be here when you woke up."

Something niggled at me, something that I needed to do, but whether it was the painkillers I had on board or the whack to the head, I couldn't think what it was.

"Them?" I asked Savannah.

She placed the magazine on my bedside table and clasped her hands together loosely in her lap. "If by them, you mean Clarke, Redding, and Mills, they've been apprehended."

"Shot?"

"Mills sustained a superficial gunshot wound to a lower limb."

"So, they're all rotten shots then. 'Cause there was a lot of gunfire." A bolt of alarm shot through me at the memory, and the machine by the bed beeped in response.

A nurse hurried in, studied the device and the spikes of my heart rate, pumped up the blood pressure cuff wrapped around my arm, and scolded Savannah. "Okay, that's enough. No exciting the patient. Out."

"No!" I reached out to halt Savannah, who'd started to rise. She sank back down. "Stay. Please. Until Galloway gets here." I turned my attention to the nurse. "My body, my rules."

She glared at me, and I met it head-on.

"Fine. But you need to rest," she eventually capitulated.

I indicated the bed. "I'm resting. See? Anyway, what's the damage? My leg is in a cast—did I end up breaking my ankle?" The force of driving headfirst into the ditch had undoubtedly made my initial sprain worse. It wasn't inconceivable to think I'd broken some bones.

The nurse held up a hand and counted off on her fingers. "Four stitches in your forehead from a deep laceration. Twelve stitches in your upper arm from a bullet wound—relax, it grazed you, the bullet didn't penetrate. And the ankle? Torn ligaments near the ankle bone and outside aspect of the foot and ankle. You'll be in a moonboot for a while."

Moonboot? Lifting up the covers, I peered at my offending limb. When I'd woken, I'd felt the weight and restriction of what I thought was a cast, but she was right. It was a huge, black, multi-velcro-strapped contraption that encased my foot and calf, stopping just below my knee.

"Well... that's good, isn't it? That it's not broken?"

"Sometimes, tendon and ligament injuries can be worse than a break." She swiveled on her heel and was at the door when she tossed over her shoulder, "No weight-bearing. Use those." She pointed to a pair of crutches leaning against the wall.

Oh goody. I could just imagine how well I'd cope with those. "Savannah? Could you?" I pointed to the plastic cup and jug of water on my nightstand. My lips were still stuck to my teeth, and I was pretty sure my breath could strip the paint off the walls.

"Sure." Savannah poured the water with precise movements and handed me the cup, straw thoughtfully angled my way.

"Thanks." I scooted up on the pillows a little, wincing as my whole body protested, the numb feeling receding. I figured the nurse had listed my primary injuries, glossing over the fact that I was, no doubt, bruised from the top of my head to the tips of my toes, not to mention the whiplash. At least it felt that way. "What does that say?" I jerked my thumb toward the notice pinned beneath my name. "It doesn't say no coffee does it?"

Savannah chuckled. "No. It's just your hospital patient number."

"Phew. I was worried for a second. Soooo..." I raised a brow. Or attempted to, but for one, I've never been able to raise just one eyebrow, and two, the stitches and dressing on my forehead was an excellent deterrent for any overzealous facial movements.

"You want me to get you a coffee?" she guessed.

I nodded. My neck muscles protested the movement, but I ignored them.

"Even though it'll be from a vending machine?"

I nodded again. I didn't care. Water was… water. It had no kick. And I desperately needed a lift. I was hydrated enough thanks to the drip in my arm, which I assumed was also delivering pain meds because my mind was still foggy. I had to do something, but I just couldn't put my finger on it, and that bothered me. I hoped caffeine would shake it loose.

Savannah passed Galloway in the doorway, murmured something to him I didn't catch, then he was sitting on the side of the bed, clasping my hand in his.

"How are you feeling?" he asked. I looked him over. Besides a graze on his chin, a black eye, and some bruising along his jaw and cheekbone, he was relatively unscathed.

"Fine." I smiled. "I feel great."

"Liar."

I tried to look affronted but failed. "Fine. I'll feel great after I've had my coffee. Come on then, fill me in. What happened?"

"Savannah told you. Clarke, Redding, and Mills were apprehended at the scene."

"Yes. I got that much. But what happened to you? When did they get you? How did they get you? Was it Mills?"

Galloway's eyes darkened, and I saw the anger swirling in them like a storm on a summer's day. "I heard what he did to you," he growled, all alpha male and sinfully gorgeous.

"It's okay. I broke his fingers for his trouble," I assured him. "If not broken, then severely dented." I hadn't missed the dirty rag Mills had wrapped around the fingers of his left hand. His right hand was cut up, probably sore but not broken. I felt a little zing of pride at my efforts.

"I'd like to force-feed him his spleen. Through his nose."

I snorted. "There's a visual. Come on, though, spill. Who got the jump on you? Was it Redding? Or Clarke? Although..." I trailed off, thinking. Clarke was the top dog. Doubtful he would do his own dirty work. Plus, he was overweight and unfit, whereas Galloway was in top shape. "It was Redding." I nodded, my head bopping continuously until Galloway gently clasped my face between his hands to stop the movement. Okay, so I wasn't altogether in control of things yet. I needed coffee. Then I'd be fine.

"Yeah, it was Redding. Knocked on my door, and I let him in. As soon as my back was turned, he struck me over the head."

"You turned your back? Didn't you suspect him? Or had he flown under the radar?"

"He was on my list. I think Mills must have been with him. Mills was sneaking around outside, made a noise to distract me. I turned to the window to investigate. Redding beamed me. Woke up in the barn, trussed up like a Thanksgiving turkey." I could hear the note of pique in his voice that the two of them had gotten the better of him.

"How were you not shot?" I asked. "Bullets were flying everywhere."

"Because none of those knuckleheads knows how to shoot. Though Redding managed to wing you." Galloway ran his fingers along the edge of the bandage wrapped around my upper arm. "Savannah said your car was found in a ditch, run off the road," Galloway whispered. "Front end smashed in. It's a wonder you weren't killed."

"I'm okay," I reassured him. "It takes a lot to kill me."

"I think the pain meds may be messing with your head." He grinned, sliding his hand down my arm to capture my fingers with his.

"I think you're probably right." I sighed, relaxing farther into the pillows. I yawned. "There's something I'm supposed to do. I was going somewhere when they ran me off the road. Only I can't think what it was."

"It can wait," Galloway assured me, his voice and touch soothing. "Just rest."

My eyes drifted shut, then I cracked one open. "You'll stay? You're not going to sneak off as soon as I'm asleep?"

"I'll stay," he promised.

"Good." I closed my eyes again, only for them to pop back open. "Wake me up when Savannah arrives with coffee."

He chuckled. "Sure."

We both knew he wouldn't.

I drifted off to sleep with my hand in Galloway's, only my slumber was far from restful. Plagued with dreams of Mills and his cohorts chasing me, guns blazing, Ben would appear and disappear, and I struggled to remember where he'd been throughout all of this. A teenage girl ran through my dreams, dressed in her track gear, hair pulled high in a ponytail. She jogged past me, waved, then sprinted away.

"Kira!" I shot bolt upright, ignoring the pain that traveled through every single nerve ending in my body, letting me know in a not-so-subtle way that sudden movements were not the best idea. "Ben? Did you find her?"

"Easy." Galloway had my hand and was rubbing his thumb over the back of it. I glanced around the room, searching for Ben. Was he back yet? He should be back. Ghostly teleportation did not take long, and he'd been gone... what was the time, anyway?

"Where's Ben?" I was concerned for my incorporeal friend because it was all coming back to me now. Kira Melendez was missing. Ben had traveled to the city to check out Michael Campbell's office and townhouse for any sign of the teenager. "He should be back by now."

"Audrey," Galloway warned, squeezing my hand.

I tugged my hand away, irritated. "No," I snapped. "Ben went to see if Kira was in the city." Oh, duh, my gray matter was slowly catching up. Galloway didn't know about my case. It had all happened after I'd last seen him at the station yesterday morning. "Kira Melendez is fifteen years old, and she's missing. No one's seen her since yesterday."

"Okay." He nodded, voice low, his eyes darting to the doorway and back to me.

I glanced over to find Amanda and Dustin standing there, looking concerned. Amanda stepped forward with a massive bouquet of lilies and laid them on the trolley at the foot of my bed. "It's probably the concussion," she said to Galloway as if I wasn't lying right there in front of her.

"Excuse me?" I said, "I'm right here, you know."

"Audrey. Ben is dead. He died a while ago." She spoke slowly and loudly, as if I were deaf. Or dumb.

I frowned at her. "I know that."

"Well, then, he couldn't have gone to the city, could he? Because he's dead."

"Yes, thank you, Amanda," I snapped, waving my hand in dismissal. That was when I noticed the takeout cup of coffee sitting on my nightstand. I leaned over and picked it up, took a sip, and spat it back into the cup.

Galloway chuckled. "Yeah, that's been sitting there for over an hour."

"You could have stopped me," I grumbled.

"What? And come between you and coffee? I'm honestly not that brave." He stood up, bent over to drop a kiss on my cheek, and said into my ear, "I'll go get you a fresh cup."

"You're my hero." I sighed.

He winked and left me alone with Amanda and Dustin.

"Head injuries can cause confusion," Amanda said, taking Galloway's seat.

I ignored her and focused on Dustin, who was standing at the foot of my bed, eyeballing the large bump under the covers, thanks to my moonboot.

"You guys," I rolled my eyes, "I'm fine. A bit beat up is all. Nothing that won't heal."

"Of course you will." Dustin grinned and gave me a wink.

"We should get you tested for any neurological deficit," Amanda continued.

We ignored her.

"So, what happened?" Dustin eased onto the edge of the bed. "A car chase and a shooting?"

I grinned. "Right? I couldn't make this stuff up." I then regaled him with the whole story, starting from Mills' attempted abduction the night before. After I was done, Dustin shook his head. I took it to be a sign of admiration.

"I guess this means you're off baby-sitting duty for a while," he teased. "Some people will go to any lengths to get out of their family obligations."

"Too much? Maybe I shouldn't have gotten shot. It was too much, wasn't it?" I laughed.

"I don't understand the two of you," Amanda said, back ramrod straight as she looked from Dustin to me and back again. "This is not a joking matter."

"Babe, this is how some people deal. With humor."

"Just because I'm not clutching my pearls doesn't mean I'm not concerned with what went down," I chimed in.

Amanda's hand immediately went to the string of pearls around her own neck.

I patted Dustin's leg. "Maybe you should take her home? Oh, could you do me a favor? I need something from home."

"Depends on what it is. I'm not bringing you fresh underwear." He pulled a face like that would be the grossest thing on earth. He needn't have worried. My second stash of coffee pods was hidden in my bedroom. No way I'd let him loose in there just in case he found them.

"No, that's what Galloway's for." I winked, and Dustin made a gagging noise.

"What can I get ya, sis?"

"I'm working a case—missing teenager Kira Melendez. I brought home her journal, and since I can't do much else while I'm tied to this bed, I may as well finish reading it."

"Sure, I can do that. And check on Thor for you."

"And Bandit."

"Who's Bandit?"

"A raccoon I've adopted."

Amanda gasped. "They're vermin. Audrey, how could you be so irresponsible?"

How could you still walk with that stick up your butt? But I didn't say it out loud, as much as I wanted to.

"Could you just make sure there's enough kibble? And shut the pantry door, although Bandit knows how to open it, so I don't know why I bother," I said to Dustin.

He patted my leg. "Sure thing. Where's the journal?"

"Ummm." I looked at the ceiling, as if the answer were printed on the white tile. "Could be in the living room or my office."

"Don't worry, I'll find it and drop it back for you. Can't have you dying of boredom."

Galloway returned, carrying nirvana in a cup. Dustin and Amanda left with Amanda whispering to him about Bandit and that he should call animal control. He shot me a look and gave a slight shake of his head to let me know he'd do no such thing. I could have reassured Amanda I was taking Bandit in to the vet for a full check-up and shots. Still, as per usual, my sister-in-law raised my hackles with minimal effort. Let her suffer, thinking I was housing a rabid raccoon.

For the next half hour, my hospital room was a madhouse. Mom and Dad arrived, as did Laura, along with her husband, Brad. Laura cried, blamed it on pregnancy hormones, but sat by my side and refused to let go of my hand for the entire visit. I'd had to switch my coffee to my left hand so I could accommodate her.

Amongst all the chaos, I kept an eye out for Ben. He should be here. Had something happened in the city? Was he stuck there, unable to teleport back? Or hadn't he made it that far at all? Had something gone horribly wrong, and he was trapped in some sort of ether world, unable to return? My eyes filled with tears.

"Hey." Galloway, who'd been leaning against the windowsill, standing back to let my family spend time with me, shoved away from his slouching position and crossed to my side, sinking onto the opposite side of the bed as Laura. Cupping my cheek, he wiped the moisture away with his thumb. "What's up?" he whispered.

A wave of emotion crashed down on me, and I couldn't breathe, couldn't speak. The room blurred as more tears filled my eyes to then overflow down my cheeks. My lips—along with my chin—trembled.

"Oh babe, it's okay." Galloway pulled me carefully against his chest and wrapped his arms around me. He was my haven from the storm, my anchor. I'd be lost without him.

With my face pressed into his shoulder, I heard him say, "Okay, folks, I think that's enough for today. She's fine, just tired. It's been a big day. Doc says she can go home tomorrow, so maybe y'all can visit her at home? She's going to need some help with cooking and stuff, so maybe you can make and freeze some meals?"

His suggestion was met with total agreement. Clever man. Send them on their way but give them a job to do so they feel like they're helping. Which they are.

After the room had cleared and we were alone, he eased me away and peered into my face. "Okay, now tell me what's really up?"

"I can't find Ben. He went to the city, but he wasn't sure if he could travel that far, and that was hours ago." I sniffed. Galloway reached over and plucked a tissue from the bedside table and handed it to me, and I dutifully blew my nose.

"He'll turn up."

Will he, though? I'd just pulled myself together and asked for another coffee when Dustin appeared in the doorway.

Seeing my blotchy face and bloodshot eyes, he frowned. "Everything okay?"

"Yeah." I sniffed and gave him a watery smile. "Just a speed wobble. I'm fine, honestly." Then I glanced behind him. "She's not with you, is she?" Heaven forbid Amanda found out about my emotional breakdown. I'd never hear the end of it.

"Nah, dropped her home. We could only get a sitter for an hour. Here." He stepped into the room and handed me Kira Melendez's journal.

"Thanks, bro." I clutched it to my chest. I needed to find Kira. It had been twenty-four hours, and for her not to call home, to at least let her mom know she was okay? That told me something was up. Something more than a runaway teenager.

"I'll leave you guys to it. Take it easy, okay?" He pointed at me, waved at Galloway, and disappeared.

"About that coffee?" I smiled sweetly at Galloway, who laughed.

"Coming right up. How about some real stuff?"

I gasped and hugged the journal tighter to my chest. "You mean, not from the vending machine? You'll leave the premises?"

"For you, yes, I'm prepared to make that sacrifice. Plus, I'm starving. We missed pizza Friday. How about we make up for it?"

"Yes, please!" He really was the best guy in the entire world. I just might marry him one day. The thought sobered me, and my face fell.

Seeing it, Galloway grinned, kissed me, and said against my mouth, "Don't stress, I'll be as fast as humanly possible."

I snorted and watched his denim-clad rear as he walked away. I'd never get tired of that view.

Chapter Fifteen

The pizza was delicious, the coffee divine, and I felt a million times better. Because I was eating and drinking with no ill effects, my drip was removed, and I was free to go to the bathroom, which heralded my first attempt at using crutches. Actually, it wasn't as bad as I thought it would be, perhaps due to the added incentive of *use the crutches or pee yourself*. Still, I made it to the bathroom and back with no incident.

Galloway dozed in the armchair while I propped myself up in bed and opened the journal. The last time I'd looked at it, I'd flicked it open to a page at random and read about Kira planning on dumping Rowan. This time, I flicked to the last entry and kicked myself that I didn't do it sooner. There it was, in black and white. Well, purple and white since Kira used purple ink, but still, I smacked myself in the side of the head for my own stupidity then winced because my head was actually quite sore.

I feel bad for lying to Mom and Dad, but honestly, they deserve it. Dad's being a total dick about the Campbell Contract, treating me like a little girl, like I'm not old enough to make my own decisions. Okay, so I might suck at making boyfriend choices—what a jerk—but to deny me my chance at the Olympics because he doesn't 'like' Mr.

Campbell? That's just juvenile. So yeah. I don't feel so bad about it.

Holly said not to tell ANYONE, especially not my mom, because she's worried Mom will steal her idea. But I'm excited to trial it. As Holly described it, Restore is a combination of the cleansing power of water with regenerative marine minerals to accelerate post-activity recovery. Plus, guided meditation for mental strength and focus. But it's not just a treatment. It's an immersive experience, with deep tissue sports massage, myofascial release therapy, cupping. Plus, a special diet and training sessions. I can't wait to try it all. Okay, so the olds will probably freak out that I'm gone overnight, but they'll get over it. They need to learn that I'm no longer a child. I can make my own decisions.

Flinging back the covers, I swung my legs out of bed and tugged at my hospital gown.

"What are you doing?" Galloway had cracked open one eye and was leisurely perusing my half-naked form. "Not that I'm complaining," he added.

"Getting dressed. Here, help me." I flung the gown at him and searched for my clothes, which were not in my bedside locker as I'd expected.

"Why are you getting dressed?" He sat up and tossed the gown onto the bed then stood and crossed to the built-in cupboard by the bathroom door. He pulled out a bag and put it on the bed next to me.

"Because we need to go. I know where my client is. Well, not my client but her daughter, Kira. She's the missing person. And I know where she is. And if I'd just read the blasted journal yesterday, she'd be home already."

Digging through the bag, I pulled out a bra, T-shirt, and sweatpants.

"When did you get this?" I asked, pulling the bra and T-shirt on.

"After I got the all-clear and you were still out of it." He shrugged like it was no big deal. But it was a big deal to me. Galloway had to be the kindest, most thoughtful hunk of *Captain Cowboy Hot Pants* I'd ever met.

"You know you just earned yourself major brownie points, right?"

His grin was sexy as all get out. *Oh, yeah. He knew.*

"Can you help me with my moonboot?"

"I'm not sure I should be aiding and abetting you." Nevertheless, he knelt in front of me and unstrapped the boot, easing my foot out. Together, we managed to slide the sweatpants on, then he reattached the boot. I did not mention that even that brief amount of time out of the boot hurt like the blazes because if I did, he'd insist I get back into bed, and I had no intention of doing any such thing.

"And just where do you think you're going?" Nurse Broomhilda, as I'd nicknamed her, blocked the doorway.

"They're going to discharge me early, anyway." I picked up the crutches and balanced myself.

"You are not free to go." She crossed her arms, and her lips sucked in, and a vision of Thor walking away with his tail in the air crossed my mind. Yep. Her mouth looked like a cat's—

"I'll keep an eye on her," Galloway interrupted my train of thought. Maybe because he was thinking it too, judging by the way his lips twitched.

"No, absolutely not. Enough of this nonsense. Back into bed with you." She hustled toward me, reaching out to take hold of one of my crutches.

"Excuse me!" I snatched the crutch away from her and almost fell over. Galloway supported me while I repositioned the crutch and eyeballed Nurse Broomhilda. "This is not a prison, and I am not under arrest."

"No, well," she cleared her throat, "you are also under our care, and we have a duty to—"

"Don't even," I cut her off. "I already know I don't have a concussion. That was the only reason they were going to keep me in overnight, to keep an eye on that. But it turns out my head is harder than I thought. I can stay off my ankle just as easily at home as I can here. And it would free up a bed for other patients.”

“You’ll need to sign a release form.”

“Be quick, ‘cause I’m outta here.” I almost laughed out loud when she swiveled and took off at lightning speed. I wasn’t sure if she was getting release paperwork or backup to manhandle me back into bed.

“Are you really discharging yourself?” Galloway raised one brow.

I shrugged. “Well, I wasn’t going to. I was going to come back, but hey, if I can break outta here early, I’m all for it.” I dropped my voice. “You know how I feel about hospitals.”

Opening the cupboard door where my bag had been stashed, he threw me a grin over his shoulder. "Got those free steak knives yet? Or was it the colonoscopy?"

"So far, it's sutures and moonboots. I don't want to push my luck."

He retrieved a pair of ballet flats from the bottom of the cupboard and approached, dropping to one knee. "Sit." He patted the bed, and I dutifully lowered myself to the firm mattress while Galloway lifted my good foot and slid the ballet flat on.

"Where are my flip flops?"

"Either in your car or somewhere at the barn. Either way, they were not on your feet when we brought you in."

And yet, he'd remembered something so mundane as making sure I had shoes when packing a bag for me. "C'm'ere." Cupping his face in my hands, I pulled him forward and kissed him, doing my best to push into that kiss all the love, appreciation, and thanks I felt for him being the amazing human he was.

"I love you," I whispered against his lips.

"I love you too."

Our tender moment was ruined by the return of Broomhilda, who stormed into the room as if I were committing a cardinal sin and slapped a piece of paper down on the trolley, followed by a pen.

"You'll need to sign this." She dropped a white paper bag on top of the paper. "And take those."

"Everything okay?" I asked, eyeing her flushed cheeks and lips pressed into a thin line.

She shifted her weight from one leg to the other and sighed heavily before glancing at her watch.

I cut my eyes to Galloway, who was watching Broomhilda, then shrugged and picked up the pen, scrawling my signature.

"You'll need to come back in seven days to have the sutures removed," she said, deadpan. "If you have a worsening of symptoms, come back here or see your GP."

"Got it." I grinned.

"Keep off your ankle as much as possible."

"Got it."

"Good luck," she directed at Galloway.

He replied, "Thank you."

She left, clearly ticked off. But I didn't have time to ponder Nurse Broomhilda's mood.

No, I had a teenager to find, and I was ninety-nine percent sure I'd find her at the Divine Delights Spa & Resort. I was kicking myself I hadn't read her journal more thoroughly earlier. We could have had her back home with her parents so much sooner.

Galloway tossed the spare shoe into the overnight bag then the white bag with what I assumed were pain meds, before zipping it shut and hooking it over one shoulder. He hovered by my side as I slowly made my way out the door.

"Where's my purse? And phone?" I asked, our progress along the corridor painstakingly slow. Maybe I should get myself a wheelchair and have minions push me around.

"I think they were collected as evidence, but I'll double-check with Savannah."

"And my car? Is it… fixable?" I cringed at the thought of my beloved Honda, crushed and dented in a ditch.

"I think so, but I'm no expert. Your insurance assessor will need to take a look."

"Right, right." My premiums were going to go through the roof. "I know you said my phone is probably in evidence, but… is it okay? It's new. I only got it this morning." I couldn't keep the pout out of my voice.

"New? How come? Audrey, what happened to your old phone? Did you drop it again?" I recognized the teasing tone in his voice and didn't want to bring him down with the truth. So, I lied. A small white lie.

"Something like that," I said.

He chuckled and shook his head. "What are we going to do with you, hmmm?"

"Keep me supplied with a lifetime of phones and coffee?" I suggested hopefully.

"That can be arranged." He winked, and I practically swooned. Saved by the elevator, it dinged, and the doors slid open. Galloway reached his arm in to hold the doors open while I maneuvered myself inside.

"Tell me about your case," he invited after hitting the button for the basement parking lot.

I managed to pack everything into the one minute and thirty second ride.

"Too bad you didn't read the journal earlier," was all he said.

"Yeah. Too bad." I already felt bad about that, and now I felt a million times worse. I clunked along on my crutches and one leg as we made our way to Galloway's car. He helped me into the passenger seat, stashed my crutches on the back seat, then slid behind the wheel.

"You've gone quiet." He punched the spa address into his GPS on the dash.

My mouth turned down. "I feel bad."

"Are you in pain?" He immediately swiveled toward me, and I shook my head.

"No, not that kinda bad. That I botched this investigation. That a teenage girl has been missing all night, and if I'd only read the darn journal, she'd have been returned home safe and sound by now."

Galloway ran his knuckles over my cheek in an affectionate caress. "Don't beat yourself up about it. You're still new at this PI thing. Mistakes happen. The silver lining here is that she's safe."

"Good point. She's probably having a ball. It's the rest of us who are freaking out."

"Where are you guys going?" Ben asked from the back seat, making me squeal in fright.

Galloway hit the brakes, and the car lurched to a halt, throwing me forward against the seatbelt and reactivating all of my already sore muscles. "Ow," I whimpered, rubbing my chest.

"Sorry. You screamed."

"Ben joined us. He startled me."

"Oh. Right. So, he's not stuck somewhere, then?" Galloway took his foot off the brake and continued out of the parking lot. Soon, we were out on the open highway, heading toward Divine Delights Spa & Resort. I had a feeling of déjà vu—I'd been traversing this very highway when Redding forced me off the road.

"Stuck somewhere?" Ben repeated, leaning forward between the two front seats.

"I panicked. I thought you went to the city and it was too far to travel, and you got stuck."

"Nah, it was fine."

"Why were you gone so long then?" I demanded. I'd been worried.

"Sorry, Fitz. I got a little... carried away."

"You went shopping, didn't you?" Ben had an addiction to the shopping channel. I could just imagine him having free rein in the city, it was impossible to resist.

"Possibly."

"Definitely."

"I checked out Campbell, though. No sign of Kira."

"That's because she's been holed up at the Divine Delights Spa & Resort this whole time." I filled Ben in on what we'd discovered. Or rather, what I'd found when I finally got around to reading her journal.

Ben placed a hand on my shoulder, the coldness soothing to my tender muscles. "Chalk it up to experience, Fitz." That was pretty good advice. "No use beating yourself up over it. The most important thing is you found Kira safe and sound."

"That's what Galloway said."

"That's because I'm a smart man," Galloway quipped, having no idea what we were talking about since he couldn't see or hear Ben.

I may have dozed for the rest of the journey because the next thing I knew, Galloway was at my door, and I was blinking sleepy eyes at him.

"Did I drool?" I asked, wiping the back of my hand across my mouth.

He laughed. "No."

"Ben says I'm a mouth breather who drools."

"Ben watches you sleep?" I heard the note in Galloway's voice. The one that said he thought that was creepy. I shot Ben a look of triumph.

"Low blow, Fitz," he said before walking through the car.

"Only on the sofa," I explained to Galloway.

"Well, tell Ben that I have it on good authority—mine—that you do neither of those things."

Handing me my crutches, he helped me out of the car, and that's when I caught my first glimpse of Divine Delights Spa & Resort. The place was a mansion! Why Holly Wilson felt threatened by Stephanie was beyond me. Holly's spa sat on acres of green, lush land, and the facade itself was to die for. I could only imagine inside was the same—a treat for the eyes. And while Stephanie's spa was lovely, it had nothing over Holly's in the grand scheme of things.

Chapter Sixteen

"I'm sorry, Holly's with a client right now," the receptionist said.

Galloway pulled out his badge and held it out. "Tell her it's important."

"Yes, sir." She stepped away from the reception desk and disappeared behind a door marked private.

"I wonder if I can get a PI badge," I said absently, watching as Galloway slid his badge into his back pocket.

"They do come in handy," Galloway said. "But to answer your question, no, PI's do not get their own badges."

"Waving my business card around doesn't get the same results," I complained.

"No?" He sounded surprised, and I laughed, playfully punching him in the shoulder and promptly losing my balance. He steadied me then pointed toward a sofa. "Come on, let's sit. You're in no condition to be on your feet. Foot."

He didn't need to convince me. I'd just lowered myself to the plush cushions when the door marked private opened, and a brunette woman dressed all in white appeared. She saw us and headed over.

Galloway stood. "Holly Wilson?"

"Yes?" Holly was pretty in a plain way. She was what I'd call average. Average height, average weight, average looks. Although, peering closely, I had to say she had magnificent skin. It was almost as if she didn't have pores.

"Detective Kade Galloway, and this is private investigator Audrey Fitzgerald."

"Excuse me if I don't get up." I smiled.

Holly looked from me to Galloway and back again. "How can I help?"

Galloway sat down next to me, indicating Holly should pull up a chair. I appreciated the gesture. I was bound to get a crick in my neck from looking up at them otherwise. After she was seated, Galloway murmured, "Over to you."

Oh. Right. I cleared my throat. "I understand you have Kira Melendez staying here?"

Holly's head snapped back, and her fingers touched her lips. "Ummm," she hedged.

"Are you aware that she's a missing person?"

"What?" Her voice rose, and the hand at her lips moved to her chest. "But she's not missing. She's here."

"Did you, or did you not, warn her not to tell her parents where she was going? That she was coming here to trial your Restore program?"

Holly paled. "Oh, my God. I did say that."

"Why?" Galloway cut in.

"I was joking!" she protested. "Well, half-joking. I didn't want Stephanie to catch wind of my new program aimed at athletes. Especially when she had her very own athlete living under her roof. You know, it surprised me that she didn't have some sort of program or treatment in place already. I didn't want to give her the idea. But I asked Kira not to mention the *program*."

"Yes, but your two establishments? They're very different," I pointed out.

"Whispers on the grapevine have it that Stephanie has a wealthy backer. Nothing to stop her from expanding."

So, Stephanie's secret wasn't so secret after all. Interesting. Had Bill got wind of it? Was that why he'd put the kibosh on Kira working with him?

"I don't get why y'all think Kira is missing, though? She's seventeen, hardly a child." Holly looked truly confused. As she should be.

"Kira's fifteen," I said.

"A minor," Galloway added.

Holly paled, slumping back in her chair. "Oh my... I had no idea... she said..."

I cocked my head. "She said she was seventeen, so you'd allow her to... what? Beta test your program?"

"Something like that, yes. Oh goodness, I can't believe this. Usually, all of our clientele have to be eighteen and over, but because this was a beta test—and I really wanted someone of Kira's caliber—I agreed to let her in even though she's only seventeen." Holly fanned her face. "I'm so sorry. Honestly, I would never have invited her if I'd known she was fifteen. Oh, her poor parents—they have no idea she's here?"

I shook my head. "None. She simply disappeared."

Holly pulled herself together and stood. "I'll have her brought to you immediately. And I'll call Stephanie to explain and apologize."

She hurried away, clasping her hands together. I watched as she spoke in hushed tones with the receptionist, who nodded then picked up the phone.

Within five minutes, Kira stood before us, wearing black leggings and an oversized T-shirt. "Busted, huh?" she said.

"Apparently so," I agreed.

Galloway pointed to the chair Holly had occupied. "Sit."

Kira sat.

"Explain," Galloway ordered.

Rather than being cowed and apologetic, Kira was defiant and decidedly unapologetic for her actions. "I lied because Mom and Dad would have said no. They say no to everything. I decided to get what I want, it's easier to cut out the middleman."

I blinked in surprise. She had a point. However, she was a minor, and her parents had a say, like it or not.

"Did you stop to think for one second that you could get Miss Wilson into a lot of trouble over this?" Galloway said, voice calm and even, whereas I was amping up to rant and rave at the errant teenager.

Kira frowned. "Trouble? What sort of trouble?"

"You're underage. Inciting you to run away from home. Corruption of a minor."

"I didn't run away. I'm having a spa retreat. And no one has corrupted anyone. Holly wanted some people to test her new athletic program on, and I volunteered."

"By lying. To your parents and to Holly. You told no one where you were. You skipped school. You stayed away overnight with no word to your parents. And you know who your parents will blame? Holly Wilson. They could press charges."

"She didn't do anything wrong." Kira pouted.

"No, she didn't. But she's the adult in this situation. And you've put her in an impossible position," I said.

Kira looked at me, eyes blazing with defiance until she unexpectedly deflated like a balloon. "I just needed a break." She sniffed, eyes welling with tears. "All Mom and Dad do is argue about the contract from Mr. Campbell. Mom wants to accept, Dad doesn't, and I'm caught in the middle. Neither of them has thought to ask me what I want."

"What do you want, Kira?" I asked.

"I want Mr. Campbell to be my manager. I want to go to the Olympics. He can help get me there."

"So, this little stunt was… what? A chance to teach your parents a lesson?"

"Maybe. But also, I'm growing up. So I'm not seventeen yet. I will be soon. And then I'll be eighteen, and they'll have no say at all."

I sighed. "I see where you're coming from, Kira, I really do, but this hasn't been the best way to go about things. Go pack your stuff, and let's have a sit-down conversation with your mom and dad, okay?"

"Fine."

My mouth quirked in half a smile. Fine. A word that was typically meant to mean everything was okay. But more often than not, fine meant the exact opposite.

Kira left, and Holly returned, worry evident in the way her fingers kept twisting together. "Okay?" she asked.

"Kira's just getting her things," Galloway explained. "But may I make a suggestion? Let this be an invaluable lesson to everyone—from here on out, check IDs."

Holly inclined her head. "Consider it done."

Galloway stood then reached down to haul me to my feet, passing over my crutches.

"I'm going to get Audrey settled in the car. Can you bring Kira out once she's packed?"

"Will do," Holly replied.

The drive home was spent in silence. Kira gazed sullenly out the window while I debated if it was okay to drink alcohol while on painkillers.

Galloway's calming presence came in handy with Stephanie and Bill, who were overjoyed at having their daughter back and equally furious that she'd pulled such a stunt to begin with.

"Thank you," Stephanie said to me again as I sat in the passenger seat, ready to leave after dropping Kira home.

"You're welcome. Good luck."

She snorted. "I'll need it. But your detective was right. Our daughter is growing up, and she has a voice she wants to be heard. This was a wake-up call for all of us."

I patted her hand and smiled then stifled a yawn. It had been an eventful day. All I wanted now was my sofa and coffee.

"When you're feeling up to it, come on by the spa. Bring your friends. Free treatments on me."

"You know, I think I will. I saw you had a coffee body scrub that I wouldn't mind trying."

"Oh, you'll love it. I can highly recommend it."

* * *

Ten days later, Laura and I pulled up in front of the Ivelisse day spa. My stitches were out and the crutches were gone, but I still had to wear the moonboot, so I clunked along the red brick path toward the historical building, my arm looped with Laura's. Mom and Amanda followed behind us. I'd decided this would be a family outing. A reward for all the looking after I'd received while recuperating.

"This scrubbed up well," Laura said.

"Yes," Amanda replied from behind us. "Stephanie has done a wonderful job."

"Looks expensive," Mom said. She was right. It did look like the kinda place where you'd lay down several hundred dollars a visit.

"Relax, Mom." I smiled over my shoulder. "It's not going to cost you a cent." Even if there was a cost attached, I'd happily pay it so Mom got to enjoy the experience.

After pushing open the glossy wooden door, we stepped into the foyer.

Stephanie Melendez looked up from behind the reception desk. "Audrey! You made it." She beamed. "You're looking better."

"I'm feeling it too. Meet my family. This is my Mom, my sister Laura, and sister-in-law, Amanda."

"Welcome to Ivelisse Day Spa."

"I have to ask, what does Ivelisse mean?" Laura asked.

Stephanie smiled. "It means life." She handed each of us a menu. "Take a look at what's on offer, and we'll get you set up in one of our treatment rooms."

"Are there limitations with the treatments since they're complimentary?" Amanda asked. "Like, facials only?"

"Not at all. In fact, I encourage you to select one of the full-body experiences."

Liking the sound of that, I flipped to the relevant page in the menu. My eyes landed on the coffee body scrub I'd seen on earlier visits. *Sold!*

Seems Amanda saw the same thing because she frowned and looked from the menu to me and then to Stephanie. "Perhaps you could recommend something for each of us? I'm looking for something hydrating. Working in an office environment all day is very drying on the skin. And I'm sure Mom would enjoy something uplifting, maybe something that will help her arthritis? Laura is pregnant, so something that will calm her hormonal skin, perhaps? And Audrey. Well,

I'm sorry, Audrey, but you just look exhausted. I'm not sure the coffee scrub would be a good choice for you."

Laura, Mom, and I looked at Amanda, with our mouths hanging open. Way to point out our flaws in one fell swoop. Laura's hands flew to her face, checking for breakouts. I leaned toward her and whispered, "Relax, not a single zit in sight."

"Thanks," she whispered back.

Stephanie blinked, her smile frozen in place before she gathered herself. "Yes, of course, I'd be happy to recommend suitable treatments." She turned to Laura. "A lot of the body treatments are not recommended for pregnant ladies. First trimester?"

"Second, but I'm not really showing yet."

"Congratulations. So, what I'd recommend for you is our prenatal facial. It's deeply-restorative, hydrating, and calming. You'll receive a gentle exfoliation, hydrating mask, and regenerating cream that will leave you with a lovely glow."

"Sounds good."

"And to go with the facial, we'll set you up with a relaxing scalp massage, foot scrub, and foot massage."

Laura sighed. "That sounds wonderful. Especially the foot massage. Even though I'm only a few months along, my feet are killing me already."

Stephanie raised her arm and waved her hand, and a woman in the day spa's pale pink uniform appeared.

"Laura, your esthetician today is Louise. She'll take excellent care of you."

Laura and Louise headed off, while Stephanie sorted out Mom and Amanda.

Mom was having a luxury lime and ginger treatment, and Amanda a lemon verbena hydration wrap.

After they had left with their respective estheticians, Stephanie turned to me. "And that just leaves you and me." She smiled. "Come on through, and we'll get you settled."

I followed her upstairs to a treatment room, stripped out of my clothes and moonboot and into the paper panties provided, and lay face down on the treatment table, a faux fur blanket over me for modesty and warmth. Candles flickered, and a soothing playlist piped through the speaker in the corner of the ceiling. Stephanie had left me alone to get ready, and as I lay there waiting for her to return, I let my mind drift to thoughts of the coffee scrub coming my way. Coffee was my nirvana. To have it rubbed on my skin wasn't something I'd have thought of doing myself. Still, hey, I was open to new experiences, especially if it involved coffee.

The door opened, and Stephanie returned. "All set?"

"Sure am."

"So, we'll start with the exfoliating first, then we'll rinse that off, and you'll be massaged with a nourishing oil promoting overall health and well-being."

"Okie dokie." I couldn't wait for the coffee exfoliation. I lay with my eyes closed and listened as Stephanie bustled around, prepping for my treatment.

"I'm going to lower the blanket to just below your waist, okay?"

"Mmmhmm." I felt her fold the blanket back as far as my lower back, then she folded it from my legs up, leaving all of me exposed except for my behind.

Then she began layering a cool paste onto my skin with a spatula. Starting at my shoulders, she moved down my arms, back, and legs. While the concoction went on cold, it soon warmed from the heat generated by my skin, and along with the warming came the smell. And what I was smelling was not coffee. This was something much more... pungent.

"What is that smell?"

"This is a marine algae that is rich in minerals and nutrients," Stephanie explained. "It's perfect for anyone feeling rundown and tired. Amanda requested this treatment for you."

She did? Sneaky little so and so. My irritation at Amanda overriding my wishes was interrupted by Stephanie saying, "I'm going to wrap you in a thermal blanket, and while we let the wrap do its work, I'll give you a relaxing head massage with organic oils."

Whatever. I was sulking because I wasn't getting the coffee experience I'd been expecting, but still, despite the smell, the algae wrap actually felt pretty good. And the thermal blanket was toasty warm, and I imagined it was doing good things like opening my pores.

All of my angst was forgotten when Stephanie started the head massage, though. *Oh. My. Goodness.* It was a good thing I was lying down. I doubted I'd have the strength to stand once her fingers started their magic on my scalp.

Days later, the massage ended. I lay there on the table, wrapped like a burrito and smelling like the bottom of a lake, one hundred percent relaxed. With the massage over, Stephanie began unwrapping me from my burrito. "Okay, time for you to rinse off."

After being released from the thermal blanket, I felt cold and soggy, so the warm shower was a welcome relief. After that, it was back on the table for a divine massage, the oils Stephanie used a welcome relief to the stench of algae and seaweed.

One hour and twenty minutes later, I was back downstairs, dressed, dazed, and relaxed.

Stephanie stood in the foyer waiting for me. "How are you feeling after your treatment?"

"Actually, pretty good." It was true. My skin felt velvety soft, and supple. The shower and following massage had rid my body of the algae's stench. Right now, I was relaxed and equally invigorated. All I needed was a coffee.

"Excellent. The others are enjoying complimentary refreshments over at the bar."

I thanked her for the millionth time and joined Mom, Amanda, and Laura, who were sipping glasses of water with slices of cucumber floating in them.

"So, how'd you all enjoy your pampering session? You, by the way, are glowing," I said to Laura with a grin.

"Thank you." First, she smiled. Then her smile slipped. "What's that smell?"

"Oh, that would be my algae and seaweed wrap, courtesy of Amanda."

Mom frowned. "But I thought you had the coffee scrub?"

"So did I, Mom, so did I." I pinned Amanda with an accusing glare, and she had the good grace to blush.

"I'm just concerned over your caffeine intake, Audrey," was her lame excuse. "Someone needs to keep an eye out for your health."

"Not your job, Amanda," I pointed out. And then it hit me. "It was *you!* You switched out my coffee for decaf!" My voice went up higher than my eyebrows.

Amanda twitched a full-on head snap that indicated she was guilty as charged. And rattled. Well, so was I, lady, so was I. No one messed around with my coffee and got away with it.

"Ladies, ladies." Laura got in between us. "Let's remember where we are, hmm?" Her eyes twinkled, and I could tell she was doing her best not to laugh.

"It's her fault I smell like a swamp rat," I gritted through my teeth. "Y'all are smelling like frangipanis and friggin sunshine."

"I'm sorry," Amanda offered.

"No, you're not."

"You're right, I'm not."

Mom and Laura looked at me then at Amanda, and then we all burst out laughing. We waved goodbye to Stephanie and headed out the door en masse, still giggling.

Amanda had given Mom a lift, and Laura had picked me up since I still couldn't drive with my moonboot. Which was no drama since my car was in the shop anyway. We stopped in between the two vehicles and hugged goodbye, each and every one of them turning up their nose after close contact with me.

Amanda pleaded her case again. "I thought a detox treatment would be better for you. I was acting in your own interests since you refuse to."

"If that was an apology, it was severely lacking. Especially in the *I'm sorry* department." The truth was, I wasn't even angry anymore. Amanda was being Amanda. But that didn't mean I was going to let it slide. Oh, no. Payback would be coming Amanda's way, no doubt about it.

"Did Dustin know about you messing with my coffee?"

She shook her head.

I grinned. "Well, you go on home and ask him what happens to people who mess with Audrey Fitzgerald."

Amanda had the good grace to look uncomfortable. "What do you mean?"

"I mean sleep with one eye open from now on, Amanda." Then I gave a cheery little wave and climbed into the passenger seat of Laura's car.

"What are you going to do?" Laura asked, sliding behind the wheel.

"No idea, but it's going to be epic!" I laughed. It was beyond time that Amanda Fitzgerald learned not to interfere in her sister-in-law's life once and for all.

"This is going to be great." Laura joined in my laugher.

"Isn't it, though? Good times ahead, my friend, good times."

* * *

Ready to keep reading **Here Ghost Nothing**? You can grab it here: www.JaneHinchey.com/HereGhostNothing

AFTERWORD

Thank you for reading, if you enjoyed **A Ghost of a Chance**, please consider leaving a review. You can find a complete list of my books on my website at:

www.JaneHinchey.com

Also, if you'd like to sign up to receive emails with the latest news, exclusive offers, and more, you can do that here:

www.JaneHinchey.com/subscribe

And finally, I'd love to invite you to join my **VIP Readers group** where you get exclusive access to me, the opportunity to win one of the monthly signed paperback giveaways, join in live videos, get sneak peeks at works in progress and so much more. You can join us here:

www.JaneHinchey.com/LittleDevils

Thank you so much for taking a chance and reading my book - I do this for you.

xoxo

Jane

Read more by Jane

Find them all at
www.JaneHinchey.com/books

The Ghost Detective Mysteries

#1 Ghost Mortem

#2 Give up the Ghost

#3 The Ghost is Clear

#4 A Ghost of a Chance

#5 Here Ghost Nothing

#6 Who Ghost There?

#7 Wild Ghost Chase

Witch Way Paranormal Cozy Mystery Series

#1 Witch Way to Magic & Mayhem

#2 Witch Way to Romance & Ruin

#3 Witch Way Down Under

#4 Witch Way to Beauty & the Beach

#5 Witch Way to Death & Destruction

#6 Witch Way to Secrets & Sorcery

The Midnight Chronicles

#1 One Minute to Midnight

#2 Two Minutes Past Midnight

#3 Third Strike of Midnight

PARANORMAL ROMANCE/URBAN FANTASY

The Awakening Series

#1 First Blade

#2 First Witch

#3 First Blood

About Jane

Jane Hinchey is an Aussie author who loves to write cozy mysteries with plenty of laughs and mayhem along the way - who says murder can't be fun? Her bestselling Ghost Detective series combines all of this into an intriguing melting pot of paranormal danger, fast-paced action, and plenty of tongue-in-cheek snarky humor.

Jane lives in the mortal realm with her non-paranormal man, two cats whose paranormal status is yet to be determined (she did catch them trying to open a portal in the kitchen that one time), a turtle named Squirt (who is massive!).

Sometimes, when the supernatural chaos calls for a different kind of story, she writes under the name Zahra Stone, where the characters you meet are as sexy as they are deadly.

Learn more or sign up for her newsletter at **www.JaneHinchey.com**

9 781922 745156